ON THE EDGES
OF VISION

ON THE EDGES
OF VISION

stories

Helen McClory

Queen's Ferry Press
8622 Naomi Street
Plano, Texas 75024
USA
www.queensferrypress.com

These stories originally appeared in:
"Atomised Ride" in *decomP* (published as "No One's Gonna Take My Soul Away")
"Boy Cyclops" in *Smokelong Quarterly*
"Conflagration" in *ESC Zine*
"Coral-Red" in *Literary Orphans*
"The Drowned Sailors" in *FlashFlood*
"Flat" in *theNewerYork*
"Frame From a Horror Film Now Lost" in *The Lascaux Review 250* (published as "Frame")
"Ipseity" in *The Honest Ulsterman*
"Limber" in *Corium Magazine*
"The Mistress of the House on the *Machair*" in *Wyvern Lit*
"Non-Insane Automatism" in *Litro* (as "tw: gore")
"Present" in *Necessary Fiction*
"Pretty Dead Girl Takes a Break" in *The Toast*
"A Short History of Creation" in *Synaesthesia Magazine* (published as "Chrysanthemums")
"To String" in *Cobalt*

Published 2015 by Queen's Ferry Press

Cover design by Brian Mihok

First edition August 2015

ISBN 978-1-938466-46-5

Printed in the United States of America

"In *On the Edges of Vision*, Helen McClory masterfully explores the slow-burning terror that exists in the space between the darkness and the light. McClory paints her scenes with carefully cropped viewpoints, subtle movements, and a strange, breathtaking stillness. This author's brilliance lies in her patience and empathy, her sure knowledge of the monsters we all fear, and, most disturbing of all, the monsters that live within us. A stunning collection."

—Kathy Fish, author of *Together We Can Bury It*

"Helen McClory knows the mysterious boulder standing in the middle of the field isn't as perplexing as what hides in the long-lived darkness beneath it. Her new book of stories, *On the Edges of Vision*, squirms as you read it, forbidding the tight grasp of expectation and rewarding the bloodshot-eyed attention of the curious. Old monsters eat here. New and strange monsters, too. Monsters with no names, and monsters with many names. You won't be able to leave this book, or its marvels, where you found them. Read and be eroded into fresh soil. These monsters will thrive in you."

—Casey Hannan, author of *Mother Ghost*

"Dark, unflinching, and utterly glorious. Every page is a surreal world compressed, every sentence breathless and bruising. From the whip-smart opening story, McClory never lets up, delivering punch after punch of gleeful fantasy shot through with the blackest humor."

—Kirsty Logan, author of *The Rental Heart and Other Fairy Tales* and *The Gracekeepers*

To Douglas, who pays my work the greatest compliment—clear-eyed attention.
And to my mum and dad, without whose love and support this book would not exist.

CONTENTS

PRETTY DEAD GIRL
TAKES A BREAK

S he peels back the plastic and gets out of the water, a little clumsy with her limbs not moving right and her blue-black blood slowshot through them. She hasn't opened her eyes yet; they've been closed that long she has to pry the lids apart with thick fingers, prop them open a while, practice her blinks. Though her sight is keen, and if there were anyone here, they'd see eyes of a glorious brightness, clear like something raised on fish and chilled glacial water. God, she needs a cigarette. Clothes first.

She climbs out of the TV and into an unoccupied room furnished with a battered tartan sofa covered in pillows and a TV table sprawled with sweet wrappers and old bills. She leaves the room for the hall, for the bathroom and the towels for her body and her hair. She should probably take a shower to rinse clean of scum from the lake, but you can have enough contact with water, you know? In the little bedroom she finds a drawer of plaid shirts and another with sweats. She gets into the clothes and, if she can't really feel warm, she at least feels something new, more going on than *body* and *dead* and *girl.*

The dead girl makes herself a coffee in the wood-panelled kitchenette and stirs in four teaspoons of sugar, plus cream, and it's the best thing she's ever tasted and she licks the foil of the cream pot before folding it back in place. There's a packet of cigarettes on the table under a cable bill, but it's not a brand she likes and there's no lighter. Well, whatever. She uses the stove and goes back to the sofa with her coffee and her smoke.

What's on the TV? Two detectives in a car, two men, eloquently snarling at each other. Countryside rolls past, low and humid and green, like a summer dying from oversaturation, or it's a city-side bleak in February. Her death is always about things other than her death. The dead girl puffs on her cigarette, slurps her coffee. Not long now. There's the sugarcane field. There's the alley. She gets out of the clothes. Always naked. She flicks her hair back from her eyes. Takes a drag and holds her breath, which she can hold forever. She mashes the butt into the table. Back into the TV. Here's nothing but a desolate space, green or stony. She picks her shoeless way across the ground, arms bound at her back. Against her throat a delicate bruise. He's killed her already, so at least there's that. And there's the spot where she's been left, right up against that tree. Right behind that wall. There's the spot where she'll be found.

Car engine in the distance. Those men, talking already. They don't ever shut up. She lies down and faces the sky, letting out slow one last mouthful of smoke.

MOTEL, DINER, ALL-NITE PHARMACY

"In perpetuity," Dan said, clutching the gallon of milk to his chest. He and Lauren had been up since last Wednesday and were immortal. Delany was in the car, too sweaty and wild-eyed to come inside. He was experiencing visual distortions. The car park was black ocean. Dan and Lauren ran out of the pharmacy with the milk and gel for mouth ulcers and vitamin C gummies and bandages and tape for the bandages.

"Did you get food for the insects?" Delany asked.

Lauren hit the gas and flung the steering wheel around. Delany laughed at the sound her hands made on the leather grip. Lauren sighed and scrolled down to a new song.

"Dearest brother," said Dan, to nobody present.

Lauren turned the music up.

At the diner they had coffee and Delany a breakdown

quieter than usual. He sobbed redly into his sleeve. Dan cut the eggs into smaller and smaller pieces. The yolk glommed to his knife. None of the three had eaten real food in years.

"Does it even have a taste?" said Dan, without intonation, looking at Lauren. Lauren got up and threw her plate into the kitchen, meaning to hit something. The plate missed the cook, hit the metal countertop and shattered.

Right about then was a good time to leave.

They peeled themselves out of the car. It was hot, and the lights over the forecourt buzzed like a bicycle wheel spinning against an eyeball.

"Shit, son," said Delany. Dan, calmest-looking of the lot, paid for the room. They piled in, stripped, and fell into bed. Afterwards, something was even more warped and broken than before. But a monster will always, always, hunger to touch.

They went back out and sat in the car, in silence. Sun would be rising soon, but then it did that a lot.

Delany decided he should drive, so it happened that they went to the nearest animal shelter. Dan and Lauren sat in the back, listless. Delany stood on a dumpster, head-butted a window and crawled inside. He came out with a white kitten. It sat in the open glove compartment, winking. Lauren wanted to give it milk, but the milk had spoiled in the heat. So Dan instead bit it, giving it immortal life.

The kitten yowled and hissed and bit Delany. Delany made a terrible sound and covered his face.

"Let the sun put it down," said Dan.

Delany said nothing. Then he said, "A thousand thousand slimy things did live, and so did I."

And drove on back to the motel.

Inside, Dan closed the curtains. Another sunrise, another to follow.

"Another, another," he said.

Lauren pretended to fix her hair in the faceless mirror. She laughed and tore out a handful of strands and stuffed these under the mattress, into the dirt.

THAT TIME YOU CUT OFF MY HAND AND THEN PREPARED IT, PRETENDING IT WAS HAM

We were standing at a bench outside, buttering bread for everyone's lunch. The mood was joyous. Harry and most of the kids were splashing about in the lake. There was a wind coming off the water, and I remember how the wrapper on the stick of butter flapped about, threatening to leave. That bright string of bunting I'd put up, an attempt to evoke the summer fêtes of home, had caught in the branches of a tree, though it went on valiantly waving, perhaps for me alone. Several of the other guests were up in the house making what they called bug juice for the children, and something with a bit more tonic and kick for the grown-ups. It was you and me prepping at the bench, and only Mia as usual off by herself in the hammock, reading. You were unpacking more lettuce, splitting it apart noisily with your hands, when you suddenly turned to me and asked, "Evie, have you ever wondered—" There was a pause as I laid a pink slip of turkey on a slice of bread.

"Wondered what?" I said. It must have been something in my tone. But I can't recall what, exactly. When I think back to the circumstances of the day, I can conjure the easy grandeur of the house and gardens; the squeals of happiness, thuds of bare feet on the dock. And you. How you wore a bright bow of orangey-red lipstick and looked so well-rested, full of an energetic, almost fevered loveliness I myself had never known. Your skin with a glow to it from lounging on a deck chair the morning before, perfectly offset by that pretty grey V-neck wrap dress you had on. You'd borrowed it from Mia's mother. It was a loan given in good spirits, on the understanding it would aid your romantic overtures towards the blithely unaware Richard, Julia's almost-ex. Those days were so nice, so relaxing. Yes, it was only the nights that were a bit fraught. You finished topping a stack of cucumber sandwiches.

"Haven't you ever wondered how it *tastes*? Now, I'm sure…" you said, a little distracted, "I'm sure they'll get a real thrill. We just have to make sure they don't catch on." I could see Mia swaying in the hammock, languidly turning the pages of her book. I was thinking, I could count every leaf on the branch above her, if I would only be left in peace to do it.

"I'm sorry?" I asked politely, "not sure I'm following." I imagined you had concocted another prank. You and all the others loved silliness, though to be quite honest it made me feel a little left out. I knew exactly what it was everyone must be laughing at when some party stretched plastic wrap across the kitchen sink, or when another switched Harry's doorstopper literary tome with a Harlequin romance no one would claim as theirs. I just didn't feel it myself. But I knew I'd go along with things, because that's what you have to do, and it's nice to see the sun of other people's joy.

You had me by the hand. I thought you were going to lead me off somewhere. Instead you lifted the bread knife. I still had no idea what you had in mind.

"Oh dear, Miriam," I said, breathlessly, "I hope it's not anything too indulgent." How easy it was for me to pretend that my heart was in it, that I was part of the group. No one was excluding me, and everyone so kind and full of smiles.

And yet.

And *then*.

Well, I do wish there had been a cleaver. Something with weight to make things a little neater, involving rather fewer sawing motions. I looked down, and the pain was really quite awful. But somehow, not as vivid at the edges as you'd imagine. Or, it's perhaps because—I think I read somewhere—you cannot actually imagine what pain feels like. Neither imaginary pain, nor pain that you've felt in your own life. Since, I suppose, that pain too has become imaginary in proportion to how far removed is the past.

Blood got all over the gingham tablecloth, but as it was wipe-clean, no real harm done.

I can very clearly recall the sandwiches though, that delicious farmhouse-style bread we could only buy in the one shop in town, crusts cut off, set down on the table inside the house, next to the fruit plate and the morsels of red velvet cake. And the scarf you gave me, scarlet, just the right colour to cover the seepage. I held my stump out of sight that whole evening, do you remember? Little slivers of 'ham' you said, pronouncing it 'han' with a carefully straightened face. And you'd been so clever as to cut around the bone with a paring knife. So really nobody could tell. Oh their expressions at the end of the night. Your raucous laughter. And my face only a little paler, a fraction more strained than usual, as I laughed along at your side.

MATERIAL

Cambion at eight years old, mouth breaking in a yawn, watched his birth-parents as they slept. And it seemed to him he looked on a perfectly kind and ordinary couple drifting together in the dark. He was glad to be their son. But on the other hand the indisputable fact of how, out the window of his own bedroom, his other parents stood together on the lawn, holding hands under the treehouse that had been built last spring.

Cambion in diligence read up on the matter, finding it to be like this:

> the *Incubus* and the *Succubus* lacking souls and thus the power to generate life—in truth all things alive must have a soul, that is, all creation outside the orders of the angelic, demonic, and unseen—are on occasion stricken with the desire to themselves generate a life. The Incubus and the Succubus who wish to thus procreate must in the first instance spur a living body to produce seminal fluids, then transport this substance to a

womb and seed it there, and let the human mother be the vessel for the creature in the womb. The child born of this queer union, in all other respects visibly human, is known as Cambion

He nodded, but still had a burden of questions on his shoulders. It wasn't said in the books if the demonic creatures loved their child, though he supposed that must depend. Certainly, every night his first-before-birth-parents would come to the garden and watch over him, their wings held spread. Their faces the colour of smashed raspberries raised aloft, their smiles confused by a thousand crossing needle-teeth. Cambion learned early to be comfortable with unease. To suck his thumb and wave his fingers at them before tucking himself back in bed, to lie there drifting between glad and utterly bewildered and alone, until sleep.

His childhood years progressed; Cambion grew a little. He was not as he seemed, not fragile, not at all as his supplicant cow-eyes and spindled, stick-aided walk signified to the people of his town. He had been made in two layers, and with two gifts: to stare into the souls of whoever he looked upon and find out what was there; and that nothing, not the greatest force, could ever knock him down. He took use of the first at age ten, in finding a church with a good priest for him and his mother to attend. The soul is most visible in the hands, in the neck: the veins delineating every cruelty. The excuse he gave his mother was a dislike of the architecture of the church itself, an intense sensitivity which wasn't that different from the one he actually possessed. Eventually there was a fine black-and-white bricked room—and a priest holding masses all drowsy with incense—that Cambion would thole.

Dips of the fingers into the holy water then forehead, heart, left, right—each time a sting like a scalding cold. Which Cambion would master, he told himself. Prayers wrapped him in a bear pelt when nothing else would cover him. He waited to be good, or to be taken by the demons. Promising himself, and resisting, and leaving the window open.

At school the boys thought they'd found in Cambion a body the right softness for their fists and insults. Cambion laid down his stick. The boys' souls were like springs of water, passing colours through, nothing silted, nothing settled yet. Every hit he took with eyes raised to heaven, while no wild jab to the gut could force him to the ground. He thought about the gorgeous taste of his own blood, about what a monster he was, that whichever boy was beating him had seen inside his soul as he could. How little he could do to stop him; he had been seen and fairly judged. The boys, for their part, meeting an immovable object, all spat scorn when they meant fear, and sauntered off to tell no one. Cambion became each boy's secret. Cambion, swollen-eyed, sucking his thumb. His weakness was relentless. The fur of prayer nestling him as he rocked on his heel. And meanwhile his first parents were busy sucking the vital energies of folk in bedrooms all over town.

When do you begin to talk of the thing that you are? Cambion figured out the difference between himself and the other children. He was the only one whose curse it was to witness and to stand. He went to church, but found the words there simple, wisdom for a human heart. The pain of holiness wore off. What invites the right words to council something so utterly else? Cambion turned twelve and went up to the high school, where he walked corridors of his own, glassy and bright. His birth-mother grew to thinking, when repelled by something in his way of being in the world, that she had raised a changeling. She held him near and sobbed his shoulder dark; Cambion her own boy, her own very self. No girl for Cambion, no boy either. Beyond the fists and kicks of those who still did not know better Cambion could not bear to be touched.

At sixteen he found a job selling Christmas trees specially potted so they could be returned to the forest. The bark of the pine he liked to pick apart in small sheaves with his nails, and he fell in love with the smell of turned earth under car tracks and the slough of the iron spade digging up saplings and patting down the soil again. Not that he was strong enough to dig, but that he could watch the other workers doing so. And wait for payment, and count, and look up with his cow-eyes at customers, staring inside them at whatever solidity or terrible gape marked the countenance of their souls.

On the third week his boss saw something in Cambion he did not like, and punched him in the jaw. For always gawking like a big dumb animal, he said. By which he meant, looking on me without censure, so that I cannot know what it is I am to you. The moneybox and ledger and the little table and chair were all thrown over on the piny dirt. Like Jesus in the temple, Cambion said, smiling in his weak fashion. The boss spat. Everyone did. Everyone ought to, really. Cambion looked at his boss properly, and saw his soul weary and cracked from decades of winter ice in the woods. The boy decided there wasn't much but to act a kindness. He let himself go limp and laid himself out on the ground, groaning until the other man soured and walked off.

Was all this enough? A lie, a violent passivity, a heart like a door creaking ajar. He felt for a moment the young saint he'd tried to be as a boy, then immediately fell to a vigorous self-loathing. A not-uncommon process in the heads of the lapsed Catholic offspring of demons. At the very least I can remain confused in my own darkness, Cambion thought, knowing it is mine. At length and with some difficulty, he rose and picked out a likely tree. He staggered with it to the crossroads to catch the bus home to mum and dad.

His parents were out at the library as he decorated the thing with pretty paper stars. He swept up stray greenery with his hands and turned on the lights. In the mirror he saw the state he was in and went to wash his tear-blacked and bloodied face.

When he came downstairs his parents were there, but in their souls he saw the other two. The demons stood within them at the foot of the stairs, bodies holding hands. Was this sins being tallied and finally called in, a family intervention?

In his double mothers' hand, a book. They held it out to him. He tugged on his sleeves, but took it all the same. It had a sticker from the local library, but when he looked inside it was full of woodcut images of goat-headed men with spines protruding, and lands of rock and flames. The mothers pointed to a page midway though.

CAMBION

It said. And there were three pictures. Three options, he supposed.

THE FIRST: a boy standing with two demons. The demons take off his skin. Underneath there is a third demon with wings. The boy-demon rises into the sky, where he sits between the worlds, observing all manner of horrors he seems too at ease to halt.

THE SECOND: a boy becoming a man. The man casting away two demons. The man walking into the desert. The man growing old, dying alone in a cave full of locusts and prairie dogs. The man on death ascending to heaven, where he must sit by the gates, curled up, to await the day of judgement.

THE THIRD: a boy becoming a man. The man bringing the two demons into his life. The man becoming immensely wealthy, sitting on a throne with many people about him, raising their hands. The man on death descending to hell where he himself becomes a demon.

Cambion looked up. He held the book between his palms. So much depended on making a choice no one had uttered to him, and on a choice that was not his, that had brought about his birth. He thought about the other children, with their souls like fast-flowing water. He felt his jaw where his boss had punched it, now swollen to an egg. What are answers to an impossible creature?

At last he spoke. No deserts, no gates, no hell, he said. A wet voice, but steady. And wanting to leave the demons with a good impression, he looked into the brilliant eyes of his mother. He saw past the sins of the human soul (which was in there dozing on a sofa in front of a quiet television set). He saw down to the demon herself. The succubus has no soul, it is said. It can make no life, yet there he stood. He plunged one hand into the chest of his mother, passing through skin and bone without harm. He pushed into the demon and groped around. Within the body he found a speck, bright like a tooth in an attic. He held it up and stared at it. Now who's having the intervention, he thought. He pointed at the incubus, indicating there was a soul inside him too, and to his own body, and to the tree, and everything in the room. Then he ripped out the pages of the book concerning himself and began folding them. He wasn't sure what to make, so with a moment's hesitation he simply cut another flimsy star.

BIBLICAL

She would get up early, though it didn't matter what early was, since she lived alone, and in a tent. Early is a term rather dependant on a roof and walls, she had discovered. It was by necessity that she lived the way she did, though not out of poverty: she had bought the best tent available, large without sacrificing portability. Made out of canvas so it would not gather condensation, so it— and she—could breathe and still be insulated from the crisp desert nights. Not breathe, exactly. Not at night.

She lived by necessity as far from human contact as she could bear. The desert was New Mexican, scrubby and grazed by bony kine, or was a smooth white expanse, or else pastel-banded and fringed with sagebrush. Best was somewhere with plentiful wood for burning. During the day she gathered it and pieces of whatever was to be had to eat. The right sort of cactus, or thistle roots. Rarely, she would allow herself a trip to the store. Usually a gas station where through traffic was common and the cashiers less likely to commit to memory a face, even hers.

Best to go before noon, before things began to get noticeable.

At night she would get the fire going, pull out her folding chair, swallow a one-two of bourbon, and sit patiently for what would happen. Around midnight, the moon might be there. At the very least the constellations, which by now she had committed to a place beyond memory, in the base of her skull, where it chaffed against her spine. She would stare up at the named points, counting, thinking, trying not to let them judge her, until she lost track, overcome by the bloom of stars, the milk of the Milky Way bleeding through.

She would feel it first in her face, where her scars would grow glassy then crumble, sugar-like, under her fingers. She had learned that it went easier if she helped the process along. She would pull until she came away in reasonably sized parts. Until she had the whole of herself in her hands. Cradling the fragments. Cheeks, mouth, the curve of her nostrils, her ears. Into the fire. Throwing up those little sparks. Her eyes she got to keep, right to the end. They would hang suspended where they had been in her skull.

Usually she went next with her feet, scratching until the flesh came away from all those bones. It was the same for the rest of her. Sometimes, she would have trouble. It's never easy to remove your own labia, uterus, ovaries, and watch them burn, even if you know that tomorrow all will have grown back. Her breasts came away in her hands.

She would kneel on her skeletal frame and peel off her back, shake to let her armflesh fall. Then the remainder of her bones would shift to grains, collapsing downwards. Her eyes, suspended a moment longer, would fall into the fire. It was the night sky she got to see last, framed by infernal light.

She hadn't always been this way. Trial, error, and fear had taught her to burn the pieces of herself, though perhaps the result the next morning did not matter so much as the act of the night before. Often she had asked herself what she'd done to be cursed this way. The only answer was, naturally enough, it was something to do with damnation. That this was punishment for being her, for everything she wasn't. She'd grown up knowing God sees from the beginning of time all the souls that are going to be damned, and so when you've done the thing to be damned for, or not done it, just felt the skim of it against you, that's it— no more heaven but for looking up at, in rue.

Still, every morning, there she'd be, waking swaddled in the sleeping bag, another day rising behind the mesas. Her body freshly hers again. In the ashes outside, crystals of the old body would glint in the aqua blue. She always felt almost—almost—not the worst creature in the known world. She'd brush her new teeth and spit in the sand, feel the warmth on her neck. Imagine kissing someone for the very first time with her just-made lips and tongue. That was the curse, too, she supposed. To be this happy for just a while. Then it was time to get back down to where she belonged, and she'd throw some new logs where the embers lay, hang the grill and prepare breakfast: boiled coffee, thistles, whatever was fit, right over where she had burned.

THE DROWNED
SAILORS

It would be best if we didn't live here together anymore.

You like the smell; that's what you'll miss. You like the smell of rot on the shore where we staggered to stay, the fumes off our mouldering tar boat huts, and the North Sea itself, cold and humid. A chill territory, a grey steppe with no heaven on any side, but everywhere to be gone. You would have taken longer to know it, if things had been different. If I were to ask you again, at the mouth of my wood stove, with my damp mementos strung above to dry, though they never would, if you would bide again on the Pacific, on that island where it was always warm and the sea was always giving its blue cracked flavour, and the people knew you, and were your people, you would say no.

You wouldn't mean it, but you would mean the gesture of saying it.

I told you you don't have the grace for oblivion, and you told me to stop reading poetry. It's not right that a dead thing should keep how to read. It's not right for the dead to miss. You muttered at me to keep quiet. Your hand running across the bands on your throat. I said fine. Just as you were leaving I hauled that fishhook out of my leg. It had been in there a long time, the flesh pale, swollen around it, and I meant it to hurt. And for you to see. Though it couldn't; though you did not look. And here I am, scrawling, after all that. I still mean all my gestures, if not my intent. Like you with the pipe smoke, though you can't taste it. The rings it makes, passing through our stubborn light.

I think of closing my eyes, of sinking into the black weeds, letting myself be pulled on the tide, against and against the juts of volcanic rock. It will do for my purposes now, to make of me fragments of form. An absence of meaning and absence of done, a lost message, finally rubbed clear of ink. A piece of mute sea glass at the bottom of a trench.

I have nothing to leave, now you've left, and only a little I wish to take. The lingering memory of your petulance. The drift of our drowning, our years living it, while the town huddled up the coast, while ten-thousand miles distant our wives slept in their twin shoreside graves.

The knowledge of your hand as you gripped me, once, warm, when we fell.

PRESENT

Coya is in the main lodge kitchen, leaning against the cool wall. She watches moths tick into the electric fly catcher at the open door. Outside there's that familiar rectangle of light, cut on the steps down. Beyond that, a square of indirect light makes a pitch of blue grass. She pays attention to anchors. This one is pretty good, steady. Out past the lawn she can see nothing but black and little lights that might be insects, or folk travelling through the woods, if the woods weren't knotted up tight, and the ground under them wasn't hidden beneath a fold of water.

She's thinking of her neighbour, Ray. Ray's tall and split with stress. He wears polo shirts that were someone else's first. A brother's or a cousin's, or one of the men who visit. But on weekends this time of year he wears special clothes for the hunting party. Red, so they'll see him in the corn. Ray is calm those days. He told her first he was a beater, but she found out the lie. Other sorts of work get better pay.

Coya's bones feel heavy. She pulls at her vest to let in some air. She's been cooking since six, and now she has to go home in the dark, alone. Ray said he'd stop by, but now she doesn't know. She runs her hand down the rib of her braid, then looks at her palm. Flour. But under it, the lines she knows how to read. Flames, death—not hers. Flames and death, huh. Her death she knows. The line for her life stops in a smudge, breaks down like a delta. She taught herself what that means, and how to put the future away when she has to get on. She lifts the vest to poke at her belly. It's like flat-top bread baked with an egg wash. She looks back out the door. The corn will burn, she guesses.

There's the sound of a car coming up the gravel. This big house, and no noise inside or out after the workers go home. Excepting when the hunting parties come for the late-summer weekends.

It's Ray; she can hear his step. The way he puts back the screen door. And she can smell him, before he's seen. It's that kind of night. Coya, he says, all smile. She just nods and picks up her purse. You got somewhere to be so fast, he asks. No, not really. Ray says, let's go for a drive or something. In the car Coya sees the Virgin on the dash, glue bulbing at her edges. She picks at it. Don't you do that to her, Ray says with a harsh tone. They drive for a while, windows down, through sugar and corn and branches. Seems that every bent leaf prickles against her skin as the light slides it into sharpness and then lets it fall. Gotta get some gas, says Ray. They stop. Coya gets out to stretch.

It's like getting a cramp. It starts in the same place, the same size. Like a pulpy fist, pushing up. She knew it was coming. At worst her eyes are a bit glassy when it hits.

She's never told about the soul-cramps. Anyway, sometimes they switch into a behind-the-eyes migraine. Not this time: she's standing in the gas station lot, then she's also standing in a hallway, looking into a room. She closes her eyes. Then she's at the fringe of a corn field, can hear gunfire. The bright day pressing on her shut eyes like a menace. The corn is making sounds, parting in long lines, and above it, in front of the lines, the birds are rising in their clamour. A bell tinkles. That's it. She's back at the gas station. Ray's paid up. He wants to go for something to eat, but Coya tells him she can't tonight. He's bought a deep-blue drink, and they share it, driving home.

Ray parks and gets out first, walking away. Coya breaks the dashboard Virgin free and slips her into her purse. Goodnight Ray, she calls back. He says, up early tomorrow for the hunt, Coya. You catch the bus, okay? Maybe you can get me some lunch from the kitchens and I'll get you for a ride home early. Yeah okay Ray, she says, goodnight. She goes into her house and washes up, then picks over the bodies of her sleeping sisters to get into her side of the bed. But there, she can't sleep. There's a light coming in the room and it illuminates her palm. Coya holds her hand against the wall for a while. She wipes her face and breathes out.

It's not like she knows, not all the way.

She thinks, her older brother has the best running shoes. He'll be so mad. But things go missing; home is a busy place. She leans to sitting. Okay then.

Outside, she stands on the dirt, barefoot, holding the shoes. Almost every streetlamp has broken, so there's only one point of light for anchor. It's Ray's house. She crosses the street through the band of nothing, opens the metal gate and pads up to the porch. Little plants, little weeds, touch her. She lays the shoes down neatly at the door and takes the Virgin out of her back pocket and places Her in the right shoe. Sorry, she whispers, and tucks the lace around, buckling Her in.

Next morning Coya wakes to the ricochet of birds in the corn getting shot at by the men from out of town. There's no cramp, not all the ride up to the big house. But that can't mean much. Her hands fret the zip of her purse, moving it in and out of the blinding roadside sun.

CONFLAGRATION

She spat out the match she unpinned her red hair she struck the panel she saw the spark she eyed the man she smirked at his pleading she counted to three she threw the match down she ran through the wheat she rushed before her hair and under the night she was chased by the flames she was chased to the stream she could not cross she cursed all the stories she snuffed a road out the fire she walked back to the man she extinguished his body she undid the charred ropes she touched his hand she brought him to life she swore at her bad luck with a voice forged from gold she said can you forgive me can you imagine my distress he said what the actual fuck lady I don't even know how I got here and raising his fine head he rose to his feet like one long-seated on a tedious journey he walked off to his car without looking back.

BOY CYCLOPS

I met my friend the cyclops for a drink at a downbeat cocktail bar with damp green walls and mismatched furniture. We went all sorts of places together. Today, he was buying. He'd recently come into some suspect fortune. He was playing tarot on the table nearest the aquarium. It was still light outside, though nearing 11 p.m. In summers in this country we have extra hours for daylight, which we steal every year from the winter months like hapless teenagers who think they know what'll work, what'll hide the stolen measure of booze this time.

So the cyclops is a boy, though a monstrous one, with his green eye very pretty and his slender hips. But his teeth are like those of elephants. The Ancient Greeks found the skulls of elephants and mistook them for the skulls of giant men, one large eye where the trunk was missing from the wide white face. He tells me elephant teeth are not the preserve of any creature. He tells me he will never die, so long as he is a creature made from this confusion, and not any more complicated. Or he did tell me, once.

I slumped onto a stool and kicked my shoes against the table spars.

"Hiya," I said, in the irritating manner of my people. He smiled, shrugged. Sometimes he won't speak for days. That day was for the cards, but he had many hobbies. Taunting the fates, reading books on World War Two, defacing public statuary with jaunty traffic cone hats.

The first time we met was in the Edinburgh Central Library, which perches on a bridge, its lower floors descending unseen into the Cowgate, rooting there in a valley of drunks and "saunas" and old piss-dripped stone. The Cowgate has been a human-enclosed valley for over eight hundred years, but the cyclops remembers when it sheltered delicate fern as broad as a cowflank, and rare and sober yellmen in skins hunted the deer and sometimes mated with them, to good effect.

The librarians in the central library are aye bent bored over their desks, being neither hunters nor deer and since digitalisation lacking cards to stamp. They carve their initials in the wood of their desks using their antlers. Their necks hang low and downy, and their collars are of the loosest cut to accommodate them. I had never failed to note how this city had accrued such fauna, though only the cyclops ever caught me at it, sidling up on the edges of vision, with a grin.

"You've only one eye," I'd said, and him snickering away in happiness at that. Not even the librarians with their velvet ears heard him, their soft-gloved hands turning the pages of Bibles, margins demarcated with illustrations of their kind.

"Now, what's my fortune?" I asked, snapping a corner

of one card, "since you've had yours." His wallet lolling there on the table, full of our pink-purple money depicting one of our many murderous kings.

"A drink, if you couldn't guess," he said. Usually, he said more extraordinary things. The world of mythological creatures in modern day is without magic yet infinitely precise. He could tell me fanciful stuff about poor people who lived for centuries, begging, forgotten by death. He could walk vertically up Salisbury Crags to wait for me at the top, tapping his Converses while I traipsed up the human way, along the path by the yellow gorse. He knew every part of the city, that which had gone in fire or been torn down, and parts that were to be. And though he could not take me there, he pointed them out. Here in 1647 a woman planted a garden that could only be seen by children. Here in 800, a prince of the Anglo-Saxon settlers was killed by a boar set on him by a Pict, a painted man. Here in 400 BC the cyclops gave away his virginity, but never would tell the name or the form of the creature. I didn't press, though I didn't always believe him. He looked too fragile not to have kept his purity. I suspected his untouchedness kept him. Even myths will lie as they please. He could be coreless as a fig, if he liked.

"All right, I'll get us drinks."

"No need," he said, and rose with a flourish. Him with his chest of plasterboard, his big soft green eye, but with tension in countenance like the front of a Viking longship. Off he sailed to pillage the bar.

"I'm glad we skip the tourists here," I said to no one in particular, to the lacy goldfish swaying to its inner musical boredom. When I turned around, the cyclops was ordering us tall plum brandies, knock-downers, dapper as you like. As you can be, wearing a small black hoodie with the cowl of it up over your curls.

But there, all in an unheimlich way, was his other eye, visible green as the first.

He walked back to me. Everything had taken on civilised proportions and nothing at all was worth a note but the burn on my lips of foreign summer fruit, and the strum of it down my throat, and this boy tilting cards, frowning primly, as if he'd never seen Death or The Fool before.

PECAN PIE

The door opens, letting in a handful of leaves, but it isn't her. Bernina folds her dishcloth. The customer removes his winter woollens and seats himself at table four, by the window. Bernina doesn't know him, and doesn't care to, but finds herself looking anyway. The stranger has fine features, perhaps that's why. She walks out with her notepad and the last of the coffee. She can't remember much, so even the simplest order has to be written down.

He curls his fingers around the menu.

"Cold tonight," Bernina says, pouring him coffee.

"You're the only place open so late. I'm very grateful," he says in a strange whisper. Although he doesn't stress anything in particular, Bernina hears a rhythm, a whole history. The voice is a foreign one, at once restrained and by its fine restraint willing her to inquire. This annoys her. There's nothing she hates more than submissiveness. Or so she thinks, tapping her toe once on the linoleum.

The customer looks up and out the window. His

face in profile, strawberry-blond hair a little curly but neat, eyelashes long. Bernina thinks, if only Marguerite were here. Marguerite starts her shift at the bakery at four-thirty, and if she hasn't been drinking the night before, she usually drops in around this time for coffee, right before Bernina locks up, indirectly handing over the shift to the morning girl, who'll get in at six. So Bernina thinks, if only Marguerite were lounging in the corner, catching her glances, rolling her eyes at the stranger's talk. After the man was gone they could make fun of him.

But Bernina has no way out of this.

Night is on the street, but dawn isn't long off. The sky is the telltale colour of the inside of her eyelids when she stands in the back lot and closes them, drinking her coffee after her shift. One car passes, lights combing the sidewalk, making Bernina shiver. She shifts her foot again and scribbles to make sure her pen is working.

"I'm sorry, I was somewhere else," says the customer.

"England?"

The man laughs. "Yes, that's right." Bernina has delighted him.

"What'll it be honey?" she drawls, which again breaks his face into a smile. She sees his eyeteeth and thinks about going to the movies with Marguerite and saying, that customer had teeth like that. Teeth that would look better with somebody else's blood on them.

Sometimes Bernina's thoughts disturb her. Then she understands everyone is on the receiving end of thoughts like this some of the time. Especially at four in the morning.

"What do you still have that's fresh?"

Bernina sets her face like she's insulted. "Everything's fresh here."

"Oh, well, I'm sorry. All right, what do you recommend?"

"Pie's not bad."

"Okay, then whichever pie's closest in the fridge."

She draws a picture of a slice of pie and retreats to the kitchen, calling out the order to the empty room. The cook went home at two. She cuts the slice herself and spoons the whip on top. She slides it through to the counter side of the window, walks around and takes it over to table four. The man is cupping his chin with both hands, his twin in the window looking hollow and lost. I won't talk to him, she thinks. I'll just let him sit with himself.

"Just passing through?" she asks.

Well, maybe he will say something strange she can then tell Marguerite. The customers who come in at four never say much that's normal. It's as if normal wears down like a battery. Four is flashing-red-bar time.

"Are you?" he asks. Oh here we go, Bernina thinks.

"Me?"

"Are you just passing through?"

Bernina inspects a frayed line off a button on her cardigan. "No, I live here."

"Have you travelled much?"

"Nope. Don't need to. I can get everything I want without leaving town. Eventually everything comes through here."

"At—" the customer pulls up his wrist to look at his watch, "at four twenty-five, I'm coming through. And so you don't have to go looking for me, isn't that right? You don't have to go to England, or walk endlessly in the wastes calling my name. I'm here."

Oh, Marguerite was going to laugh. A great big cackle, like she does when something really gets her good. Or else she was going to be speaking to the police about the last time she'd seen Bernina. It could go either way, but Bernina figures she'd take her chances. She can fight, if she has to. She imagines holding her fist with one hand and throwing her elbow with all her weight behind it into the stranger's face.

Bernina turns, "I'm getting you more coffee," she says, shaking her head. She busies herself with the counters, waiting on the coffee to brew. There's her phone in her bag. She picks at it. No new messages.

She sees the man rubbing at his face. Two faces: the eyelid-coloured reflection on the outside of the window, and the flushed narrow version on the inside. He sips his coffee and angles his fork like he doesn't know what it is for, only that the light looks good on it. Then his palm is on the table top, rubbing it like he's thinking, where is this, what does this table feel like. The corner of Bernina's mouth twitches upwards. There is no sign of violence or sleaze to him. Maybe only the regular measures, and that you have to forgive. He is speaking and acting weird because it's late, because everything is wearing down, and by rights he should be in bed. She is supposed to be locking up. Her shift has finished, but you can't leave with a customer there. Unlike in a bar, you can't tell them you don't have to go home but you can't stay here. The bounds of hospitality are drawn differently in a diner.

She finds herself walking over with the coffee pot and a cup of her own.

"My shift was supposed to be done like five minutes ago. I usually have my morning coffee before I lock up."

The man smiles and holds her eye. He doesn't blink much, but the light wavers there, making the gaze soft.

"I know," he says, "I mean, I bet that's what you'd do. That's what I'd do."

Bernina nods.

"In fact, I'd make all kinds of contingencies, if I were you, if I were alone with a customer I didn't know."

"Yeah. A strange guy could do just about anything. I have to know how to handle myself."

"You'd—fight dirty. You'd elbow me in the face."

"Yes I would," Bernina says, laughing a little.

"You'd—relish it. I think," the stranger says.

Bernina raises her fingernail to her mouth to chew on it. Something hangs crooked between them, making the hair on her arms stand up and the air taste strange, floral like blood.

"What's your name?" she asks.

The man laughs. Right now, Bernina likes it better than Marguerite's. Maybe when the sun comes up she'll think differently. But right now, she likes the wistful way he has, the way a laugh can fit the moment, just as layered and complicated. The man has still not started on his slice of pie. Doesn't look like he's had much of his coffee, if any of it.

"You aren't hungry," says Bernina.

"I'm miles away."

"What's your name?" she asks again.

He looks up at her. She sits down opposite him and fills her cup. He's watching her, but it's not the kind of look she expected. She wonders what kind of dance this is. Maybe she's been tripping over her feet, and he's too kind to let on.

"It'll just make it harder on both of us."

Bernina purses her mouth. "Huh."

Again he laughs: apologetic, embarrassed, reciprocating, sly. She looks down at his fingers. They are inky. But more than that: the tips are black, like they've been dipped in ink, or tattooed, with the black grading to greyscale dots at the second joint. The man draws his hands into fists, then lets them shoot out, wiggling them like he's performed a trick too fast for even the result to be caught.

"Are you the devil?" Bernina asks.

He looks surprised. Then he frowns.

"Have some of the pie," she says to him, grabbing the little spoon from his side, "I'm going to help you with it, so we can both get our job done."

"Nobody's ever caught on so quickly, Bernina."

Bernina puts a spoonful of pie and whip in her mouth and closes her lips around the metal. She makes a small sound and shakes her head.

"I just want to get my shift done. I always end it with coffee. Let me tell you a secret though. This pie's way too sweet. Too sweet to be right, but good for times like this."

He laughs again, so that part's not pretence. It is a very appealing laugh. His reflection in the window laughs too, one beat off.

"Sooner or later, everything passes through here," Bernina says, "one devil or another." She pauses, rubs the residue from her lip. The skin feels rough like butter spread thin on a square of toast. "You, though. The nicest yet."

She says it weightless, reaching for another spoonful of pie. She thinks very hard about nothing, though the edges of that nothing throb tenderly. The devil cups his inky hands round the coffee and drinks it down, long and slow. His throat is beautiful, breakable. Whatever he'll do next she'll do right back.

A car sweeps down the street. Light gleams on the plate and on the surface of the coffee and in the devil's soft eyes. Bernina thinks, whatever he'll do next, she won't ever tell. Some things you got to keep for yourself.

AFTER HESSE

The village, Dunmuir, is a monster and it always is.

Since the defendable outcrop on the hill was first sighted, the clear stream found, the first stone pummelled the first wooden post into position, it has always been. The square flowered where the market had shambled, and it was a wicked thing. It was not the living and the dying of the people that made Dunmuir monstrous, nor the deeds of its citizens; the cholera and the witch-burning, the acts of public shaming, the stubborn criminals who found ways to lurk in a space three streets by two across, the loveless old-folks home. Nor that incident in 1986 in the abandoned school bus on the edge of the haugh. Nor, indeed, the many poisonous inequalities in the systems which hold the village of Dunmuir together—these, it is true, were mandated far away and long ago and are little understood by the natives.

The village caused none of this, contributed only a little grit to the discord and sorrow of its inhabitants. It is a monster because it has had thoughts since always, when it should not have, ever. It watches at all times: a neutral, closed grey eye, an uncracked oyster. It sprouts and withers across its hill like slime mould, drawing out its boundaries and then crossing them. But more than any of these common enough monstrous demarcations, to be clear—the village always is.

What does this mean? That the stars may drift overhead, loosening from their orbits and the predictions of astrologers who carry on saying, soothing, the stars were as they were, and so are you bound to warm fates. That though there are many universes in which you are loved by your beloved whether you are both jackdaws or the first and last lines of a favourite poem, either way, Dunmuir exists. Even when the blueprint of some of these universes does not permit the formation of villages, these universes are, nonetheless, never without *this* village.

In our world, Dunmuir sits on the hill in stone and street and flesh activity, with moss where the Northern rain plumps it. Over time, various randomly allocated progressions cause the market to fade into obscurity. The tracks of horseshit, too. Fashions and forms of speech alter. A corner shop grows, full of macaroni tins and cans of vitaminised energy water. Lights come on in the evening in the windows: promises, signals, small breaths (all these, in fact, the same thing). Cigarette butts outside the village's four pubs roll here and there in secret, like the small notes once carried by pigeons.

But in every world, under any combination of stars or their utter absence, under flames or primordial darkness, with love or without, Dunmuir is to be found, more or less as it is here, though sometimes the air of the world is too toxic to sustain its human element.

How Dunmuir makes itself, how it secures continuation, is not to be known. Nor what it wants, this monster. Sure enough it is a limited sort of creature, given it cannot move far. Given that it seems to want for nothing. To exist, stonily. To disquiet to a certain degree. To notice that the linger of a hand on one of the older walls is in its weight a pacifying gesture. To feel the wreath of poppies on the war memorial is laid so, not just for the dead. And in that it is satisfied. Passing at speed through all worlds like a flipbook, as you do, this is the best that can be offered; there, and there, and there again, Dunmuir.

FLAT

Tennen is drinking on his dock.

But he isn't. He's playing at drinking on his dock by looking at a photograph online of a dock on a lake in America, a country he has never visited. But he has had beer. He drinks a Pilsner on this dock, pretending it is his. Not everything, just the dock, the beer, perhaps the shadow from a little property behind.

In Tennen's country it is dark, and this he likes. He's waiting for the train to howl through his town, a thing it does only at late points in the night, sporadic as stars. It howls and this, even though it is sporadic, stitches the hour so that it sits flat.

Tennen wishes for his country to become flatter and finer-grained, like linen becoming cotton becoming sand the colour of pure limestone. He likes to think of this as happening without any unravelling, a smooth process. Once he put a small fox or a dog to sleep by pressing his palm against its throat, because the small fox or dog had been run over—at night, so he couldn't tell which canid it was—and it was suffering. Tennen had not run it over, because Tennen cannot drive. The two of them were on a long quiet part of the road. Things needed to go white and there was no other help but his. Or, it was necessary to do it with no other help but his. It might not have been a small fox or a dog. It might have been any sort of thing, he thinks. The depth or texture of this thought, Tennen does not know.

Sometimes, if he has the energy, he gets up very early and tramps into the woods on the edge of his town. Tennen hopes for snow this coming morning because then he can stand out on the woodland path and imagine the forest getting whiter and whiter, and the sky too, and the town in which he lives, has always lived, until nothing.

Sitting on his dock, Tennen closes himself off from his nameless country whose borders he has for now smoothed out. Across the other side of the lake, he thinks he can see a person. It's a man, an old man, sitting on the stones and holding a piece of driftwood across his knee. Even at a distance, Tennen knows this man is an outdoors sort of old. He has no top on, and his arms look comfortable where they are, resting against the branch. People sometimes say a shock of white hair, when they talk about hair like this man has. But Tennen has never heard anyone say that in real life. A shock of white hair. It's strange to see an old person not being radical or styled or pitied or in some way constructed on the internet, Tennen thinks. Here's just an old man, being himself.

Tennen drinks from his beer tin. His eyes itch. There might be pollen or something blowing off the lake. In through the window of the room in which he is sitting. He is glad that the old man is sharing his safe presence on the far shore of the lake. The train howls and the blue light that has always been filling the room washes over Tennen, over Tennen's fine, ashy hair, over his soft clothes. Tennen holds up the tin and looks over the rim at the old man and decides he will salute him this way: closing his eyes and with a simple nod and a sip. He thinks, I am here to drown myself. After my beer I will slip into the lake and drown in it, once the old man is gone. Or he thinks, ah, it sure doesn't get any better than this. Another phrase he has never heard or overheard anyone say.

FRAME FROM A HORROR FILM NOW LOST

It may be unwise to linger here. Her upstairs will be passing by, presently. Which means passing through you, if you've taken a fancy to the hall and not gone out towards the extremities, beyond the French windows, into white light. Don't you notice the metallic cast on everything? One hand resting on the banister, as if it will help you with grounding. This frame is only some parts surface: a matter of break, a silver flicker. A single exposure in which to recall these early days of cinema, the wonky art to the confluence of props and light and your form. Speaking of which, you can feel it, can't you? Even if you must, at the script's insistence, pretend otherwise—feel the flow at wait, the timeless shimmer of fever.

How we know the place holds monster: hints at tensile continuities, flimsy guesswork, that class you took in queer theory—this is all it amounts to. Look. Her upstairs is monstrous like those of a silent German Expressionist film. And this monster is disjointed, raised flickering at the limit of the still; the other end is the garden, implied safety. Until she gets up to crane down through her walls, sweeping, glaring into your ringing nervous system, whatever tricks the cinematographer will grant, and, with her beautifully blacked-out lids widening, she will, descending, declaim, through a white text on the black:

'*night*'

LIMBER

Four boys run together along the sodden woodland track. Soon one of them will be lost. It has been raining in Maryland for the whole month of September. Even the mushrooms have drowned. Thomas runs at the head of the group. He is strong, stout but leggy, his body undecided on its final shape. The second is Kush, who is taller than the rest, and thin, and stooped. It is his character that is yet to be fixed. Alfie runs like clockwork, never any faster or slower than the pace he sets himself. The final boy, too, is putting in a good show. Titch pants and wipes the snot and rainwater from his face. But beats, stomps, punches the air, to the next black tree, to the one after that, keeping line of sight on Thomas' blond head, though he can't hope to catch up. It doesn't matter; what matters is getting to the other side of the track, and to Kush's, where they will pull off their shoes and clothes, shower, fold pizza into their mouths, play Xbox.

Titch is running to make an impression, but he is not sure what kind. He's new, but he's not afraid. He never will be, not at his core. Even as he shakes from the effort, from everything getting slicked down, so that even his eyelashes struggle to keep up. The puddles deepen. He's splashing through muddy water, through the leaves falling on his shoulders. He trips, scrapes his knee, and blood flecks as he gets up limber and runs on.

The wood darkens about the boys.

Alfie lets his clockwork run down. He feels something missing in the space behind him. Titch is gone. Forget him, says Kush. Probably turned back.

They'd played a game walking out to the woods after school called 'how will you die'. Thomas was going to go out trying to punch a bulldozer. Kush, falling down a waterfall. Alfie would die in his sleep. And Titch? The other boys didn't know him. They couldn't agree: death by football? Mathematics? (they knew he couldn't throw, couldn't count). A phone buzzed: Kush's dad. Home, alright?

Alfie, Kush, and Thomas stare into the woods, breath steaming. Kush is first to shout. He has a little brother. Panic squirms. Thomas is cool, steps out a few paces into the brush. Alfie cups his hands around his mouth to amplify his calls.

Later they will walk to Kush's house. Thomas will be the first to speak up.

Meanwhile, Titch stands in the darkness.

The woman comes out of a tree. She looks like a white branch, with black marks like kisses or eyes all over her arms. Her hair is stained and clinging. Her feet—he would say, if asked, there were no feet—don't touch the ground. Titch looks at his own mud-covered shoes, knowing he must be polite, even if he wants to throw up in fear, from the burn in his lungs from running. He can feel her staring down at him, about to say something. She holds out a long arm. There's a small wet bag in the nest of her hand. A pouch. The kind for sunglasses. I don't think that's mine, he says. Sorry.

She holds out the bag until he reaches up and takes it. Behind her appear more women, all willowy and damp. The sisters open their mouths. Inside he sees only black. They open their arms. It doesn't matter the details. No one will listen. Titch learned this young. He's not afraid, but he has the scars. On the backs of his legs, in this body of his that fails to thrive. He could run, though. He opens the bag. Inside it are several new things. A key made of wood, worn slick. A knife with a short hooked blade. And a tiny glass jar in which he can see four drops of blood. His own, which the woman gathered after they were spilt. He opens the jar and spoons the blood out, wiping it on his shirt. He crouches and puts the bag on the ground and the knife and the key on top of it. There is a sound of branches relaxing. Can I leave you? he says, quietly, holding his hands so they seem loose at his sides. The rain falls louder. The forest disappears around him, until there is only the patch of soil on which he stands. Above him, fresh, heavy leaves begin to fall.

SHADOWS

Can we be Cupid and Psyche? It's so terribly dark here, in here, closed in by the nothing, beloved, I sink and switch. But here comes the odour of herbs growing on a stony hillside. There are galaxies that are nothing but hanging gardens of scent. I think, and there are your fingernails, digging in the dirt and ripping leaves. The mass of it all. If I can try to describe them. Shuddering past. If I zoom in on the almond nails and the delicate green needles.

Down further is the bridge of plant veins, the cellular heartland. Down further, the palace in the mountains. The doors part and the palace is gilded but just as dark, so what is the point of goldwork and marble escaliers you cannot see? I ask, awaiting a serious answer. By the light of a candle, that's all you get. A candle held up against multiverses of sovereign black.

Can you drip wax red onto my bare wrist and that way, that way block me out? Patter. To be in love you must have a mind and a wound too fresh to measure. You must be distinct from the chaos, even if you have to wind yourself into existing. Eventually blown wounds like ridges in billion-year-old stone can be understood, having submitted to time. Something without hurt is inexhaustible. So on that scale we've not yet started. Split something atomic, shield your scalded eyes, and I'll whisper our passion. Everywhere you walk I walk even if there is no where to. Suffering, hinged.

Next, our skins must go upon the fire. This is ridiculous, the whole hag-lot, but—kissing your cheek, if my lips can locate it—I said we've not had the eons yet in which to lay out the rationale. So, muddle-kiss, your wings my wings. Your atoms swap with mine, and with atoms of wax. I saw a film about us once; I'm sure it was about us. Documentary or fiction, that's an important question. Surely if we are named, if we are Cupid, we are Psyche, then we can't be monsters, even as we cleave to each other? Contranyms are a cheap trick. They repulse me. I twixt. Anyway, at last look up, my dove, where there is so much. I'll be sliding overhead amongst it, weaving a cape from our burnt hides, our singularity, a blush peony, singing all the low notes, and you the high.

DOMESTIC GODDESS

The mother is sitting in her living room with a chrome bowl in her lap, creaming butter and sugar and listening to online radio.

Across the town and over the dunes, the sacrifices are sleeping. Sunpeeling and salt-puckered. They'd write a play about her if they could only remember how to type. It's fine to be ambitious when you are loved. Some can stand being fictional, since it happens anyway.

The song changes to something classical. Something worn into a gilt groove. She sighs, but nothing creases her placid face. The batter takes flour, two eggs, and a pint of blood. The mother closes her eyes. Inside her is insect, whispering barn, stakeout at the state-run Catholic school.

A figure in a full dress with cherries on it walks across a vista of blowing sand.

She stands at the foot of the resting surfer. Clutching the knife like an anecdote at an awkward party. Can I just? Take something from you. A canapé. He smokes and rolls his blue eyes. She cuts, thinking of turtles hatching and never making it to the cool sea.

Later the surfer will grow back. He gave us fire. He gave us his boy brilliance and some romantic poetry semi-sung in a quavering voice. Of course he'll never be sacrificial. It's the mother that's the monster, smearing a track of footprints blackly across the dunes.

Fifty minutes gas mark three.

Wire cooling. Some unbeloved band that makes a lot of money quietly beat up their acoustic guitars. A piece of Lego is carefully placed on the stairs. A bead necklace made of one's own coyote-teeth laid against the line of collarbone.

And then to the buttercream, and rosewater and crenelated castles and her words presumed taken for the hysteria of a haunted governess. Outside the girls, having woken, are singing at the tops of their voices, breaking them apart because they don't know. When they do, it'll not be her fault. A robin sings in spite. The mother spreads the layers and sets candles in hoofprints. It's a birthday. She cuts the heart out of that cake and watches it slyly bleed.

    She raises a slice and stops up her smiling motherly mouth with a tampon of grainy sweetmeat. And in the

sea all that's wilder roughened by being let to live
unmonsterly

gets gradually further from her arms.

TRYPOPHOBIA

"Fml. Think it wd be a good idea to kill everyone in this room?" the first man texted.
"What. Whatever," replied his friend.

The first man took out the gun from his back pocket. No one was looking. He hated that. It made him want to tear at his face and scream. Instead he stood up in the cinema and fired the gun into the air.

When he shot the first one, a girl, the screaming began. He told the theatre to shut up and lowered his eyes to his phone. "I'm doing it," he wrote. "Want in?"
The second man was at home, smoking a joint and looking out at the street.
"Naw, busy rn man."

A moment hardened and became something indelible.

The second man heard the shots, a joke, a car backfiring, nothing to get up for. Meanwhile a hole was punched in a shoulder. A hole cracked in the side of a skull. Blood slop flicked outwards, moistening the velvet seats, dyeing a clean shirt red. The first man rolled the bodies down the aisle and loaded another clip. Took aim at his temple and filled his head with a final round of applause.

Rallies were held. Families in silence were handed potluck plates with food that filled their mouths until they spat it out into toilets upstairs. Flowers left in tribute rotted into slush. A hundred-thousand words were written. The dead killer's name, over and over. Men far away made a good case that nothing should ever change.

The second man tried to map the holes in the world. He felt constantly sick. But he had to keep looking. He had a picture of his friend's face, the one the school had given the newspapers. He pulled it out daily and stared at it. One morning he began pushing at it with a ballpoint pen. Pushed a neat hole. The eyes gazed back. He pushed again and poked them out. It was still a face, but now something could live in the holes, some burrowing insect.

Had there always been an insect living in his friend's face? He couldn't know. The back of the picture had a story on it about a lawsuit. Now the holes had eaten into that too. He pushed the nib through the words *million* and *whiplash*, *infant* and *2014*.

He kept pushing, taking his time, choosing which words had to go, and checking where they lined up on his friend's face.

Sometime later, his phone buzzed. He picked it up; the light caught on the side of one of the holes, and something inside it twitched back.

Lights screamed outside, blue and red flashes. There wasn't any noise. He had no rights to this, to the power of obliteration. He brought out his own gun from the locked drawer. For years he and his friend had practiced in the woods. The first man took great relish in striking poses while he shot, the second man remembered. Flourish, aim, squeeze the trigger. The bottle would burst. Laughter. Sometimes, the chest of a small bird.

It was dark; the ambulances had moved on. The image of his friend was studded with holes, and the things within the holes twitched the lines of their antennae when he looked at them from the periphery of his vision.

In silence, the second man took up his gun.
In silence he began his task of stripping it down to its solid, unexpungeable parts.

ART

The boat rowed out over the sun and the depths. After forty minutes, the old woman raised a hand to her eyes. Her Ruth was at the cave mouth. The boat glided in and together they pulled her up. A white body set against the black rocks. Ruth had her arms folded for a while, after they climbed the little hill together and unpacked. There was a smell of beer in the cabin. Beer and seabirds. Mina, tired, waited with her newspaper for the thaw.

What are they saying in there? asked Ruth at last, trying to take it by the crease.

Coffee first?

There was a crunching of the gravel outside and the sound of something cropping the crisp shore grass.

Coffee on the stove undid the stench of solitary boozing.

It was all I had left, said Ruth.

Well then. Shall we go out to the porch? said Mina with a clap.

They sat with their coffee mugs, Ruth on the bench, Mina on the jute rope spool.

The island was shaped, to Mina's mind, like a whale drawn by medieval monks, half cat, half livid fish. There was a fresh spring and some rocks, some mossed and some barren, and three ancient birch trees that washed their hair in the water at the far point of the tail, where the island broke down. Ruth had made colour charts, one for winter filled with careful lozenges of greys and yellow, and the one for summer illuminated by dabs of periwinkle, raspberry blots from the raspberry cage, and many sorts of green. These charts hung in the downstairs room of the cabin. In the upstairs were the bedroom and the bathroom. In the bathroom lived a large black spider, kept to temper summer flies.

From the porch, the two old women could see the grass and the vegetable patch and the path through it. And beyond the patch, down to the inlet and the bright choppy water of the bay.

Mina took out her silver cigarette case and looked inside. Then she put the case back in her windbreaker pocket.

You don't want your lighter? You're saving them until after dinner, said Ruth, with approval.

He's eating again. Mina said, nodding towards the inlet.

Ruth nodded. Grass mostly. But he does like to get into the roots.

The shape down at the shore was a little like that of the island's, but smoother and rubbery white. It had legs and arms and a fat snout with the mouth invisible below. At that moment it was gnawing on a woody carrot, the leaves bunching in front of its face.

Mina sighed. It was ugly, always there, like a child that never grows up. Crying like a child too at times. It wore Ruth out sometimes so that Mina couldn't stand it. But it had also lived on the island longer than she had been visiting.

Mina got up and fetched a new bottle of whisky from the cabinet, adding a splash to her coffee. In the meanwhile, the creature had fallen asleep on a puddle of sand between the shore rocks. Its belly rose and fell.

He's always going to be here, said Ruth. Well, until the day I punch my ticket.

Until you sail off across the sea forever, Mina said. Yes, I know. I wish—

Mina wished her story was the one that Ruth told. She wished there was no mainland that had to be gone back to. She wished, sometimes, that Ruth was not the brilliant artist she was, so she would not have to live here, making her art away from distractions. She wished that the creature would die. But not before Ruth, she understood it could not be before that. Yet she pictured herself wrapping the creature in jute rope with heavy weights attached and rowing it out to the deep part of the bay and shoving it overboard. And peering over the side into the green slapping water as down and down it went, until it lay on the sea floor, drowned. She pictured with great callousness Ruth's heart shattering in her chest when she was told.

The sun was sinking. Ruth went over to the other side of the island to gather more driftwood, even though there was plenty in the box. Mina watched the creature. The creature, blinking into alertness, watched her. It raised a hand. Was it waving? With such things, it never does to presume. Mina's coffee was finished. She went inside and closed the door, and sat inside, looking out, until she couldn't see it, whatever it was doing, any longer, because the island was completely dark.

THE BLOOD/INJURY
PHOBIC

I sat on a table stone breathing heavily, picking at rosettes of lichen that grew upon its surface. It was winter and the grasses and weeds around the graves had submitted to frost before they could die back. I looked to the moon for a point of reference, and it did very well. But I still could not catch my breath, even knowing that a futility. I washed my hands, looked down at myself washing them with nothing but the frigid air. At length, and having no alternative, I stood weakly and went back over the churchyard wall, across the white lawn, and indoors, letting the great doors shut behind me.

The boy was still flushed and rumpled and unconscious on the chaise longue. His wine glass had slipped from his hand, the wine spilt on the flagstones. A dark red that made me flinch. I breathed into my clasped hands a while. I touched my teeth. Sharp canines that would cut me if I pressed. I crooked my finger away. The fire was roaring, and I went to stand by it. What helps is to think of a meadow, in spring, when the grasses are long and lush and there is a gentle wind soughing and sun dappling through trees. But there the boy still lay, small imprints on his neck. Where I had tried before.

I moved closer; I knelt beside him. As my eyes closed, he awoke, and with such a tiny frisson that I did not notice until I had pressed into his flesh as hard as I could bear, until my teeth punctured his skin, and I began to drink.

Now, he said, rubbing his eyes, what is it you think you're doing?

I pulled away in my shock, though I knew it would be well to keep suckling as I had always done—there was no halting the movement once begun. As I tore back, a spray came from his neck, and he, drowsy, murmured his distress. Frantic I pushed a pillow against the wound. But the blood still came. I could taste it, my eyes wide in my head, my monstrous eyes that must have had the lustre on them, displaying to him the full wooze of my need, of my paradoxical repulsion.

Thick red gushed in a torrent. The boy said no more, his body twitching. In anguish I called out for the servants, though of course there were none. At night I must send them home, for what would it do for them to see this? As the blood coated everything, I breathed ever more erratically. The pillow dropped from my hands, into the void. The last I felt was the cold dent of stone upon my head.

It is not often told of what happens when the vampire faints away before completing its kill, when it cries and wills itself to stop, until the mechanism of its body, against the furore of its demonic animation, finds a way to do so. But I was to learn first-hand. When I woke, there he stood. So bright and calm—he had changed into my clothes, some of an older style than was fashionable, but from which I could not bear to be parted.

Ah, he said, are you alright? Can I fetch you something?

I sat up, finding myself on the chaise longue, where the boy had so recently and closely been brushed by the wings of sister death. He came to my side, smiling. There was a darker patch on the fabric; no other trace remained of the great violence. What could it mean, I asked myself. There had been no exchange—no chance at a new life.

He bent to push back some of my hair which had been disturbed in the fall, then helped me to my feet. The sun was shining outside. He drew back the curtains—and in my state I was too slow to stop him. But in the sweep of brilliant light I felt no pain. I turned to him, still unsure of how much he knew. Though, what indeed, did I know? In fact, there *had* been an exchange, of a kind so complex and rare that we hardly have the words to speak of it, at least honestly. It draws around the tongues of speakers a membrane of thickest censure. Perhaps we do not want to reveal it, fearing on exposure to the air our yearned-for, unspoken truths will vanish like the morning vapour between the trees.

Looking on the boy standing upright and utterly impossible, I was struck by the remembrance of kissing, of sex, these acts which I had so long ago forgotten. I stood looking at the boy's handsome face in profile and thought about desire, which for decades I had known only as a sickening sort of hunger. It was too early and I too fevered for clarity. The boy looked out, over the wall to the churchyard: over beyond he knew of a meadow I had only seen in the dark. It was there he took me, walking at my side. I was still afraid. In truth I always would be afraid, of his miraculous survival, of my own awful capacity, which I know more of than most men do.

It was winter, the grass brown-tipped and frosted. But the scene was delightful in its own way. The trees wrote themselves against a brilliant sky, and a cloud of rooks rose with their great intelligence. How much had been forgiven, or why, I could not even begin to understand. How a weakness of mind or character had brought on this gladness. The rooks lifted in black ardour and flew over the woods, and the boy walked with me. And I understood that, whatever else, my blood was my own, and that everything held, and my heart, and his.

THE ISLAND BEYOND THIS

She'd made a feature of her haplessness, since that was the option. Fluttered her jumper at her chest. The knife lined up in the flabby belt. And at the jaws of the sea, a meeting point. Where a basalt cave makes the shape of an imploding organ, and the aurora sends green flashes over the cliffs. Night. Froth barely breaking.

Wave, breath, wave. Something like silence with a song fastened behind it. And out in the swell, the bone shimmy of a long fin. Every living thing luminesces, but there are some that might make an art of it. She crashes the sea and swims after. It glows as she kicks and muddles closer. Sees the length of her now.

It croons, as they'd said: *it's you I'll skin.*

She reaches, coughs saltwater. The lone knife, and its cutting edge.

PINK GLITTER

Grace unscrews the white lid and pulls out the dripping tiplet and applies the polish to one nail after another, then holds the drying almond surfaces up to the light. Fleck and aura of colour against the ceiling, the slow chop of the ceiling fan. Tonight's the night, though it's not tonight yet. There's music on shuffle: a mix called MISANDRY+PINK GLITTER. She doesn't know what misandry means, but it sounds tough and cool, and Grace, thirteen years old, very much wants to be tough and cool. It's hot in this island city. Sticky-hot. She's going out to Mass first with her grandmother, because it's a fast day, the wake of the feast day, and there will be an ash cross on her forehead which she won't wipe off when she goes to her friend Maricel's house. Her fringe covers the cross anyway and if she rubbed at it, her grandmother would get so sick-sad. She's been that way too much lately. It can't hurt.

At the moment of consecration, the small church begins to sway. It's an earthquake. A few missals fall to the floor like they're ducking for cover. Small shock, nothing that could stop the rites. Nothing for Manila. The priest doesn't even break to look alarmed.

After the Mass, Grace says goodbye to her grandmother in the car. The driver takes her on to Maricel's house, a beautiful villa with flowers growing up the wall, and in the garden to greet her a pure white bulldog known as St. Michael, but only to the girls, when nobody's around to hear.

This afternoon, there's few around to hear the antics the girls have planned. The cook is in the kitchen making a big salad, without meat, and cutting some fruit for a punch bowl. She doesn't come upstairs. Maricel's mother and father are on holiday in America, visiting her mother's sister. Maricel puts on her playlist and Grace starts dancing. Then they pull out the hair dye, blue for Grace, pink for Maricel. Snarking clever stuff at the TV, they sit wrapped in towels with masks on their faces, before changing for dinner, eaten in the elegant downstairs, and after, running back up to try every new item of clothing, Grace's playlist blaring again. There's a brief descent into a squabble over one of the songs. The girls coming out the other side through the power of mango smoothies, which don't count as sweets. Maricel tells a secret. Grace touches up her lipstick after brushing her teeth.

It's St. Michael who saves them. Another earthquake is coming; he wakes first Maricel on her queen bed, then Grace on the pull-out cot. Growling and pacing towards the door. Tonight's the night. They go out into the garden. The sky is low, orange. Pulsating clouds, or a trick of the eye. There's the idea of neon signs somewhere flickering in reflections on a damp pavement. A strong smell of *dama de noche*. Maricel's garden is big enough that no part of her house will fall on them if they go right beyond the pool.

The two girls stand in their nightdresses, barefoot on the manicured grass. Nothing happens. Maricel looks at St. Michael and he looks back, frightened. Well, she asks.

There's a low rumbling. Grace feels it in her stomach, a note too low to be heard. The ground begins to shake. A palm tree makes an awful noise, and in slow motion falls into the neighbour's garden.

Then, with a sudden wrench, Grace realises the shaking is coming from her. From somewhere deep inside. The ground underfoot splits, soft turf cracking along the lines where it was rolled out just last month. Maricel is watching her now. Your eyes, God, she says. Grace can only put her hands to her face. She feels the rumble intensify, as if prying her open. She tilts her head back and feels this intensity vomit out from her, straight up and into the sky. A bolt of lightning a bright pink colour, sparkling with glitter.

The noise rises in pitch; no longer earthquake or thunder, it zips past the extremities of human hearing. St. Michael falls to the ground kicking, foam at his black lips. The power spreads across the clouds. Grace can see nothing—the thick light is pouring from her eyes now. It doesn't hurt, exactly. But she's not happy with the situation.

As soon as it had begun, it is over. Grace drops to the ground, panting. Maricel stands a while in shock before getting on her knees and touching her friend lightly with her fingers, afraid to catch whatever it is Grace has. Grace spits into the grass, then reaches out to hold Maricel's hand. Soon the girls are hugging, crying, shaking. The sky continues to rage pink and gold. The clouds open; a five-mile radius of pink-glitter rain falls. The felled tree bursts into flames and is immediately put out by the heavy, lurid shower. Ashes glow like fireflies; neon-yellow, rather than the orange of true embers. St. Michael whines and gets up unsteadily, retreating inside.

All this is a beginning. But for now it's limited: only a wrecked lawn, the palm, and, across town, the church where Grace attended Mass earlier that day, chained in the gaudy lightning. Inside, the leftover ashes have all returned to bright glossy palm leaves and burst like a striking octopus from out of where they are kept. Even now they are unfurling on the tiled floor and crawling out under the door, into the jasmine-scented street.

ATOMISED RIDE

S matter on the street corner. A godless sun overhead. Police are here already for the remnants. Claw marks chalked in the sidewalk. A body consumed and wiped away from the mouth with a delicate back of the hand. Is it too obvious? Out of all the celebrities, that the most monstrous should be her?

In fact, the intel is wrong. Lana isn't the monster. She was just first on the scene. She wiped sweat from her face, mussing her lipstick in shock. As the police bag what's left, she hangs back against the wall. Her broken nail peeling against stucco. Eyes unblinking into your dodging gaze, those false lashes as needles reading her cheek. She murmurs, *I followed him here too late. I know where he has his nest.*

The two of you go to the nearest bar. You buy her a watermelon crush so cold the glass mists. She takes a long sip through the pink straw. *I lost my record producer at a party one night.* One spot of blood on the balcony, another on the stairs—and she'd followed a muffled squealing down to an unused part of the house. *I pushed open the door. He was ripping her throat out with his teeth. Too busy to see me.* She looks up, picks a fragment of ice from the straw. *Don't think I won't follow him to the end of the world.*

That's how you and Del Rey come to be stalking the bad man together.

Body after body. The nest moves around. You hire a car; she won't be shooed away. So you rent a couple of motel rooms outside Fresno and LDR sits humming above the ice machine, makeupless and sharp to any movements. She salutes as you pass her with a bag of brown-bottle supplies. Cars below her slide through the vacancy sign.

Next day, twelve hours in the saddle, the GPS beeps, and the car cuts into the sidefat of Salt Lake City. He's gonna eat a Mormon, Lana says, first words she's uttered in hours. Mostly she sat barefoot, crossed-legged, playing with the stereo and listening to radio plays. Weird pieces from the Forties you could hardly follow through the static.

Ms. Del Rey, you ask, wanna catch something to eat? She shakes her head. She points towards a Holiday Inn on its empty, spick-and-span forecourt. *He's in there*, she says, raising her head, *third floor.*

The door caves quick under your size-thirteen boot. Inside, a room lit like no Holiday Inn suite you've ever seen. Neon-green fittings with wavering light like under a bridge in some dirty place. Is that a pool in the corner? Petals float on the surface. Some other junk bobs. Wallets, watches. In a warp of shower curtain lies a half-naked man, knocked out or what. He doesn't look like much. You turn to Lana, see her eyes all brimming with neon and pool trash.

That's him, she says, stepping forward. Somewhere between the car and the Inn, she put on a white pineapple-print dress and five-inch heels made of glass. You open your mouth, pause, say, you sure, Ms. Del Rey? He's out cold. *Uh huh*, she says, licking her lips.

Lana grabs the monster by the scruff, slaps him once, neat and hard. Then she pulls a thing from her bag. It's dingy leather and long, birdbeaked. When she puts it on, you figure it out. It's the mask of a medieval doctor working through a plague.

Still wrapped in the shower curtain, the monster wakes. Lana looming over him, one finger pressed to the end of her lipless mask. Oh God, he says, trying to get his clammy hands free. Even you're backing away. *He's not here*, she says, airless. *I hear you don't get along these days anyhow.* She misquotes herself, and you just look on in piss-fear admiration.

Lana kneels, turns her head so the beak doesn't scratch anything. Puts one soft hand against his chest. The man stops shuffling. From her bag Lana pulls a chunk of white rock and points the sharp end down, above the monster's chest. Pushes aside the plastic.

Anything you want to say? she asks.

I'm sorry, the man says. He breathes in, ragged: but I know what I saw.

He's silent after that.

This is for all the rest. Lana, calm, raises the rock, straining under the weight, and brings it down, and raises it, thumps it, again harder, and again, again. Until the monster's ribs crack, are broken inwards, until the cavity created there fills with atomised red.

There's an intense smell of pine resin in the air, like the ghost of a tree. Lana drops the rock into the hole in the body. It dashes to powder, clouds with the red. There's a slow dissipation into the room's AC. Lana unbuckles, removes, and tucks away the doctor's mask. She lifts open the man's mouth; slides something out.

After, you follow her down the plush, cool hall. Ms. Del Rey slips that something into her bag. A pink oblong of crystal, but it's too smooth. Yes you have questions, sure. Ms. Del Rey takes off her shoes, humming some melody under her breath. Some eerie poise in the way she, lighthearted, shimmies ahead. Little toe prints on the carpet. And that smell of resin that follows you, invisible and fierce, out into the treeless heat.

IPSEITY

There was an emblem on the floor upon which she stood, a charm that tired her unbearably. In the fireplace, the fire hissed. Down the chimney, a storm spat. The walls of the room were mirrored and on the ceiling was a painting of the man she would marry, standing in the grounds of his home. The lawn beyond her own room was endless. She was supposed to be wealthy; she was supposed to be a princess. That's what the girl told her. But she didn't have a tiara, and no one came to remove her clothes at night or put peas under her mattress to test her. She didn't leave, she didn't eat, and when there was a sky, there was only the navy-blue lunges of Swan Lake playing on an endless loop and her furious dancing with her hands held above her head but otherwise no grace to her at all.

Toys cannot be cruel. That's a lie as much as aspirational princesshood is a pre-capitalist relic, but amounts to much the same hunger for contemporary soothes of prettiness and worship as does buying an imitation of a dress your favourite film star wore. The ballerina was a part in the clockwork music box. She only wore one dress and it was her skin, too. She was, then, a metaphor. Or a tension before the metaphor is fully realised, since metaphors are a form of violence: smashing two or more parts of the world together that would not otherwise touch. A metaphor is a hybrid in language, a monster impossible in a world where things are just as they are. It is a creature of a world of ambiguities. Who was the ballerina made to harm?

Or, who is to be cruel? It is not possible for a budding metaphor to think for itself. When the girl was fourteen, too old even to play the music box out of lazy nostalgia for the song, she left it under a chair and let the dust cover it, soft as grey snow. The ballerina felt inside herself a heart where there had been none before, tears on her face where they had never flowed before. She pulled herself up from her emblem—at great cost to her feet, which from that day on would be irredeemably cracked and ugly. She stood up on her bed, upon which she had never slept, and pushed at the tin roof until it opened a crack.

She had been made real by the force of story. Its hunger for a central figure. She had been made to harm herself with humanity. Is that also what the monster is, in part? This question is not rhetorical, because it needs to be read. The ballerina, unaware of any of these discussions of selfhood, fable, and monstrousness, climbed out of her room and stood stiffly upright if slightly crooked, tiny and hopeful and humble and brave, looking about with her dainty black eyes: the story, as it needed to, had stapled her to the world with adjectives. The desire was to find out what a roomful of ballerinas all dancing the same way looked like. The desire was to hint at the promise that there would be love and a place to find some kind of scarring emotional denouement and then beyond that a place of rest, as there might be for any of us.

But the ballerina was too tiny a thing to make a story of. In any case her story had been elaborated upon and told many times before. Hence the mirrors which penned her in, in case you missed them—an Easter egg also overlooked: the *Toy Story* logo on the plastic blanket on her bed. And so she lay down, helplessly meta, helplessly outmoded as a metaphorical commentary on reality or fiction, discarded, in fact, upon the lawn that was actually a rug, in the world that was actually a rather pleasant fictional teenage girl's room, pointlessly animated and unable to will herself to further life, or make appeals to the story or the reader of the story (hello, can you help me?). And at last waiting quietly, dumbly crying those brand new, impossible tears, the ballerina fell without moving towards the inevitable loss of consciousness, as the story dropped off altogether.

THE MISTRESS OF THE HOUSE ON THE *MACHAIR*

A black line along the floor where the rolling pin fell and cracked the tiles. The servant boy stares at it a while, breathless. Behind him the breathing, curtained windows look out on the endless sandy meadow of buttercups and daisies, the phenomenon known as the *machair*. The servant boy in his smirched apron washes his hands but does not pick up the rolling pin to place it somewhere safe. He abhors its slippage. Why had he been holding it anyway? There's no pastry needing rolled. Bread's in the airing cupboard. Her ladyship the ghost isn't conscious this early. The hearth is dusted. Everything beyond that is yellow-white *machair* and a strange, echoing pain ringing about his heart.

So he goes and makes a gin and syrup for the mistress, and a tea for himself. He puts the gin drink in the fridge with a daisy in it. Daisy for her, though he forgets: is a daisy toxic or not? He imagines her struggling to raise the glass to her lips, the constant threat of spill. It's a long time between now and dusk. He wonders if the flower will turn the faint green of the cocktail. If the pattern on the bread will please her; if she will pretend to swallow a bite or two. He drinks his tea black and another and another until his heart kicks free of the strange, echoing pain for the moment, for he finds even the slightest turn towards malice tiring, and is glad to leave it behind without having to go anywhere at all.

In the cabinet is the palette of stage paints. He clicks them open and begins painting the bones in on the backs of his hands. Next he will make a yellow skull of his face, shade in the bones of his neck. The process takes about two hours. The mistress by that time will have finished her toilette and be sleeping in the solarium, on the black floor. Not that anyone can tell except the servant boy.

Desire, he thinks, enters the mind through the skin.

People who say it is through the eyes are mistaken. Or they are mistaken in what desire is. Desire is the brink before satiation. The servant boy desires the edge of the window pane as he rests his hands on it to dry. He desires the field of flowers, where he will go to take in the morning's washing now that the afternoon has drawn out the steam from the clothes and left, in exchange, the smell of summer, the residue of pollens, the tiniest and many scents.

His hands dry. He leaves with his basket. He folds the clothes with bone-hands, with his long, long fingers. The paints are fixed so as not to smudge, still, he cannot now wash the skin, not until the morning comes.

Otherwise the ghost will weep at him. She does not like to be reminded of their difference. That he is alive, and she is dead. She wants his life, but not her death. She doesn't like to see him at work, either. To be reminded that she is mistress and he is servant. The doors click heavily behind him when he enters one room or another, and there are paths he will take specially to avoid being seen, before the time he is called on to be seen.

Now, what else is to be done before dusk? It is a high summer's day, and sundown will not be until after ten. He takes off his floury apron, which he had forgotten. He goes into the conservatory and pulls the blinds, so she won't glimpse him if she chances to look down from her bedroom window.

He sits down amongst the lashings of plants, reading a book he had left there the evening before. He won't eat or drink from a glass. If needed, he'll rub a thumb down the humidity of the leaves, chew on the vanilla orchid blooms, keep going with his teeth until he can't feel much more than their soapy sting.

The day turns and a glow suffuses the west. When he took this job, the servant boy knew all about desire. Now he knows all about it the way a leaf knows the desire of the snail rasping at its surface. He touches his face and feels the wetness of the conservatory all over him like slime.

Sometime around nine, a restlessness takes him wandering. Though the appointment is not for a few hours yet, he dresses in the clothes the mistress prefers, a tailored suit that fits his frame close, a top hat he holds like a box of his belongings. When he took this job, he would never have guessed. He had always been courageous, but nothing had ever been asked of anyone like this.

He returns to the glass room to sweat and crumple, since that is a human phenomenon as much as any other.

There is not love. There are hours to be kept. He's paid to mind the house and to be a human presence, so she, sometimes, is permitted to forget. Ten o'clock, the disc of the sun touches the Atlantic. And it's like something cutting into him, now, pushing in, as if he is the sea, forced to turn gold by a faraway, incomprehensible presence. She lies still, above him trying to read, trying to wait. She is hollow as a light behind a curtain. He sets the book down again, gets to his feet, wipes his moist face, turning and turning his hat. There is a voice, but it's his own. He hasn't spoken to anyone but her in months. He's saying, *the door.*

He steps across the room, out, into the kitchen, and opens the back door, and holds it. The field of the *machair*, the wildflower-on-sand, spreads before him, low and impossibly sweet. The village is two miles, and any ship in the bay will receive him. For everyone knows who he is, even if they only saw him the once, as he came.

He steps down onto the *machair*. He walks out. No longer the servant, now just a boy. With no luggage, as in the beginning. He, with slow breaths, extracts himself from the house, this much is all that is possible, for the moment. The grandeur of the building retreats, conceals itself behind the rolling hills. Buttercups and daisies smack against his ankles. He makes a crooked wake of bent meadow grasses. His bone-fingers let the hat drop; it rolls away behind him.

The mistress of the house hears nothing, since now
there is no one left to hear.

ENCOUNTER WITH A SMALL WITCH

You've arrived late off a red-eye, hoping to catch Iceland at its best. You've in mind: the lagoon to wash away all your cares, a glacier walk, a pony ride. And yet, you're only as good as the last man you killed. You take their power and their face.

You idle at baggage arrivals. There is an elephant circling on the carrousel. It is light grey. An elephant is not your choice of weapon, but it is the one assigned to you for this mission.

You haven't been sleeping; there is someone else to do that for you—she hasn't been sleeping either. She is a small girl with light-grey eyes. The elephant is an elephant-shaped, human-sized bag: hers. There she is, sitting alone on a row of light-grey chairs. A light is flashing and it's flashing like a fish swimming in a fever. The carrousel is rounding, an asphalt road of carnival ooze. There's the bag and the little girl walking alongside to catch it, clutching a toy dog. The girl is in light grey, with light-grey wavy hair. The dog is a darker shade of light grey. The dog looks limply over at you: you haven't been sleeping lately; the toy dog never rests. The hour, though empty, is voracious.

You walk towards the girl and reach out your hands, as if you are going to strangle her. You do this about ten metres from her, walking neatly and fast, eyes swimming in circles like panicked fish. Several avenues of intention are closed off to you now. You're only as good as the pressure your hands contain. You're only as good as the right way of saying so. You just want to take a dip in the lagoon; you've always dreamed of doing that. This is your mission. Light-grey linoleum scuds and squeals as you walk on it. With your arms outstretched you trip and fall, knocking out one light-grey tooth. The girl comes over and pats your head, then places a hood over your face. The ribbons tickle your chin. You shut your eyes. The cloth has no colour. There's the noise of the elephant-shaped bag being unzipped. You are rolled into it, and the zip done up firmly over your clothes. What a failure! Never mind, friend. You are walking inside the elephant-shaped bag.

Now you are shaped like an elephant, with crinkly neoprene skin, and you are parading around the airport. Every time you take a step the light-grey dog yelps and nips at your elephant heels, and the little girl laughs. You're not entirely sure if this turn of events is to the good, because you can't see, and you're an elephant, an assassin, a casual traveller. You find several avenues of resistance are closed off to you now: this is the power of a small witch. But the sun won't set at this latitude, at this time of year. The parade continues out into the post-midnight dusk. Circling away over the heathland, you hazard to suppose. The hour, though voracious, is empty. Never mind, friend. The thermal waters have been assigned to wash away all your cares.

CORAL-RED

Miriam's house has featured in several stylish magazines, both print and online, and it tickles her to know that across the globe photos of the interior are being shared on social media websites, accruing hearts, comments, raised thumbs. Right now, though, the house is haunted.

The children gather at playtime—after meals, before bed—and walk together between the walls. Sometimes they bicker, sometimes they sing fragments of song. New songs only out just the year before, and which some of the younger ghosts must have taught the rest. Because some of them are new, they are capable of bruising the walls with the grease of their pink palms. Miriam sighs and asks the cleaner to keep an eye out for products that will shift the stains without harming the finish on the paint.

Miriam is in the sunroom, cutting flowers. An opulent arrangement, sent by a client or an admirer. South African plant, she thinks, raising one stem, though in fact that is only a guess. She doesn't care to check. The children are walking up and down the stairs. Up and down, and what kind of game could that be, other than one to get on her nerves, specifically. She had always wanted children. And it is in part her fault they are here.

She pushes a blue thistle beside the gloss of eucalyptus. Another photographer is coming round shortly. There is a smell of coffee brewing. Very fine coffee, not that Miriam can tell. She puts down the scissors and looks through a pane of glass to the garden, to where the rain is falling steadily on the marble fountain and the overgrowth of bushes. There is no diversity of colour beyond green and white, and this is how she likes it, very well. Indoors the predominance is towards neutrals, accent colours when necessary. Except in her bathroom. This has been redone recently with a living wall, so that when she showers she can lean into mosses and ferns, seeking what she cannot articulate clearly, but which they so readily lend.

Her blood is sweet; mosquitos love her, so Miriam is careful to keep the screens maintained on the doors and windows. She used to be outside all the time, and now that she has brought the best of the outdoors in she has no need to battle with the worst. In fact, she rarely leaves the house. In fact, she never leaves unless compelled. There is something terribly wrong with Miriam, and there has been for a long time, but she has no friends to gently tell her this, and the housekeeper Ofelia doesn't see it's any business of hers. And in any case has not troubled herself to peer into the wrongness, to push her head into the depths, where she would be crossing the boundary she has drawn between herself and her employer. Things must be maintained. Or structure, blood, selves, lost.

It's raining a fine mist in the upstairs bathroom when the photographer goes in. He doesn't seem to notice. Nor, when he is admiring the sleigh bed and Amish quilt in the guest bedroom, hear the voices calling, playfully this time. Here the visual notes are lavender, mint. As if for the digestive soothing of visitors. Visitors she no longer expects, or has cause to invite. Miriam used to be so wild in her youth. She just hadn't realised it had been her youth. That at thirty, forty, she had been no older than a girl. Good friends, homecooked meals, nights on the dock, swimming under the moon, hangovers spent watching the food channel, drowning that little boy, deep-cutting the other and calling it accidental. How many accidents there were in those days.

The photographer wants to see the wine cellar. It's been extensively improved since I inherited the place, Miriam says, putting her hand on the small of his back, her jaw aching, her tiny feet in coral-red satin house shoes, as they both descend the stair.

MAN AND WHAT

Once upon a time a girl and a boy met and fell in love. It was as easy as writing this sentence; a process as common as and even less understood than the electricity that pulses without cease through our homes and electronic devices.

The girl had a ribbon around her neck, a very pretty black velvet ribbon, which she would never take off. The boy asked her about it once, but since she made it clear she would not speak of it to him, he dropped the question and never raised the matter again, though of course he thought of it often, even going so far as to touch the ribbon one time when she was asleep, though he felt terribly guilty about such treachery.

The girl and the boy lived together a while and then got married. Their life together was rich and dull, wondrous, small, penurious and sweet. They grew up and out and, eventually, old. All the while, the velvet ribbon remained on the girl's neck, though it never grew faded or frayed. When it became clear that the girl, now a woman advanced in years, was going to die soon, she asked that her husband do one last thing for her. Or rather, she was going to do one last thing for him.

When I die, she said, you can take the ribbon off. But not before. And so she died, with a little discomfort, but without much fight, in the bed they had shared. And the boy, now a man advanced in years, duly removed the ribbon from the throat of what had once been his wife. And then her head fell off.

The husband drew back in shock and grasped his dead wife's arm. There on her wrist was another ribbon, one he had never noticed before. It was the colour of her skin, and thinner than the ribbon at her neck. He reached for the scissors and snipped—her hand fell from the wrist, bloodless. He picked it up. It was the left one. There was her wedding band—gold with a tiny sapphire. Under the ring was another ribbon. Snip. The finger fell off. He looked at the other fingers—each had a ribbon. One finger after another fell, and so to the thumb. He put down the stump of the palm and turned to the headless, one-handed body that lay in the bed.

With scrutiny, he found and severed all the major ribbons that had held his wife together. After this was done he began to sob, but could not leave the body be. There were, he found, even smaller ribbons, some as thin as veins, others as fine as the finest line of spider silk. As he snipped, his wife broke into smaller and smaller pieces. He cried so loud that the neighbour next door heard through an open window and sent for an ambulance. When the matter had been recorded by the hospital authorities, the police called and the scene analysed, the police dismissed, and the husband evaluated, diagnosed, treated, given time to rest and finally released home, many months had passed. The wife was put in the ground, in a grave tied round with a black ribbon, as per her instructions. At the funeral with a special police escort, the husband had felt moved to inspect the grave for further ribbons, and had been restrained. A brief relapse, the doctor said.

Back at home for the first time since the ambulance crew had taken him away, the husband, for want of anything else to do, went to make himself a cup of tea. In the cupboard where the tea things were kept, he found a long brown hair. He raised it to the light: there, around the hair, was a tiny brown ribbon, far too small for him to cut. So he opened the kitchen window, put the hair on his open hand and let the breeze take it as far as it could. It did not fall very far. Into his own garden, where he lost sight of it, or made himself lose sight.

After that, he made two cups of tea and drank the first, watching the other steam and eventually grow cool.

NON-INSANE AUTOMATISM

The first arch leads into a second, then a third, vault-roofed, with small slit windows and those massive flagstone floors smoothed by centuries of shuffling boots. Outside, palms of snowflakes are feasting on the statuary and dissolving into the pond. The sleeper walks smoothly down the corridor. He holds a mouthful of blood behind his teeth and white lips. He's wearing a cape made of a blue and pink floral bedsheet, the kind now only found in estate auctions or pinned against windows in abandoned prairie houses. A blackened beam, a strip of horizon, the rattle of nothing waiting for the season change to let it swell and fall.

The lines are all excellent: the boy's shoulders held back like a dancer's, his step measured. The walls persuading him forward. The flow of the cape from which only his fingertips emerge. As he walks, blood oozes from his mouth and spatters the floor. But, with mastery, not his clothing or body. He is going to kill the man he will find in a room at the end of the stone corridor. His mind affixed to a guiding, velvet principal. That of the sort bestowed by a picturebook saint or a scrambled instruction for the building of a metal chair.

He stands in a bedroom with a scarlet spotlight on the bed. Progresses to the bedside. One slowed in a dream, one graceful, delicately layered, and murmuring in his sleep. He raises his fist. In the fist a Murex seashell, in colour vivid pink and white with small spiny knobs like a vertebra of a dragon. In the bed—who is in the bed. Whatever in the daytime, only this at night: a calm fatherly face on a pillow with reddened hair tucked back. The boy aims for the eye behind its plum casing and slams the hand down, once, cracking through orbital bone into smut.

The boy spits the remainder of the blood. Edges the shell to the perfect 90. Coverlet, crime scene, discarded blood-food. There is the sound from above of two thousand books dropping off the bookcase and onto the library's wooden floor. He takes off the cape, lays it on the bed, and rolls himself inside it. It is a field of flowers and a spring morning sky. He is a veal foal, a hedgepig, a syncopated man dressed for iron weather. He curls into sleep behind fluttering, bloody lashes. From up inside the angular, spinal shell, a brain's last memories spurt, coral and fearless. A wet hand limp in his, caked against the sheet.

A COMMON ENOUGH THING

He is a sandwich, with googly eyes and a big smile on his torso, long crust-coloured arms and legs. He forgets: is there cheese in his filling? His bread is very detailed to show the moist crumb. He has been a sandwich every morning for the past four weeks: padding the pavement and waving, even when there is no one to wave at. Dancing when there are more than three people but less than five coming in either direction so that he can safely perform his single move.

"Ha-ha! Look at yon man in a sarnie-suit. What a twat."

He tallied insults one of the days, but it started to get to him. Today, he has not meant to keep count but knows that he has been called a twat four times, fanny twice (by a group of school kids), and he *thinks* cunt the once (it was something muttered in passing and hearing is difficult). Wow, he wants to say, original. He's had fair time to ponder the poisonous relationship in this culture between sandwiches, genitalia, and minor alfresco displays of a corporate, commercial nature.

This instance is one too many. This is the final kick in the teeth, he thinks. He hasn't yet received his first pay as a public sandwich and the sun is powering down in a way that most other people are enjoying. So after a few seconds' wait, he skulks away, going in the direction of the man who called him names. He follows him home, as discreetly as an oversized sandwich can manage. Not out of rage: out of a bland, compulsive desire to follow him. To, after following him, confront him and have him explain just what had happened in his life to make him think that it was perfectly fine to insult people who were only just going about their job and trying to raise awareness of sandwich availability in their neighbourhood.

The man goes into a tenement building, but it doesn't seem like he needs to unlock the outer door, so the mascot waits a beat before following him inside. He stands in the central stair, craning up at the spiral. But it's the ground floor, he's sure of it. He waits again, listening. Flat two, someone's picking up their post. Okay. He rattles the door. It would be pointless to knock with gloves so thick.

The door opens. The man stands holding the doorknob, looking out at the sandwich-shaped mascot.

Quite quickly, as if he was somehow expecting to be greeted by this sight, he says, "And what d'you want, eh?"

The mascot pushes him inside, and steps after. A fight begins, with the sandwich at an advantage. No blow can get to him, and the other man is in serious danger of falling backwards. The sandwich mascot grabs him by the lapels and shoves him into the living room. The man is yelling while the sandwich mascot retains an eerie calm, aided by his absence of facial expression beyond googly eyes and a smile. He points to a chair, and gestures for the man to sit. The man throws up his hands but capitulates.

The mascot walks into the small kitchen and opens the cupboard under the sink. The man is yelling but as if towards a TV upon which he can see a politician talking cheerfully about matters with which he violently disagrees. From the small toolkit under the sink, the mascot selects a medium-sized hammer.

Later, he walks home, still in his sandwich suit.

He doesn't much notice the faces on the street around him, but fortunately they are few, and most see only a trudging, dirty sandwich mascot, a vision which makes many of them laugh, some out of mild amusement, some out of malice.

He goes to the bathroom to wash his hands, forgetting that the hands he has are gloved caricatures of hands. He nevertheless scrubs them hard with soap, and watches the red water drain away. Then he steps, with difficulty, into the shower, and stands there, impassively goggling. Water runs down the moist crumb and the fake ham slice. Water runs down the drain, taking away the last hints of blood and viscera.

A day and a half later, the sandwich, which has begun to smell, turns himself in to the police. The zip on his back has rusted shut, and he hasn't been able to eat or drink since he left his home to go to work two days before. Unfortunately, no one at the station can work the zip either, so they simply cut a small hole where they hope his mouth will be to enable him to hydrate and speak clearly.

On cutting through the foam, it is discovered that the foam is, in fact, mouldering bread. Behind the mouldering bread is an inset of slimy lettuce, followed by cheese, and a dank meat substance too aged to identify. On the other side of that, more bread, and, finally, empty air.

The officer with the scissors, a woman with over thirty years in the profession who had recently been demoted to desk and costume-removal duty, shakes her head. As if she too had expected to see nothing but sandwich where a man should have been, but is disappointed, nonetheless, by the cliché of the actual occurrence. The sandwich sighs, turns round, and waits to be walked back to his cell

SEXUALLY FRUSTRATED MERMAIDS

Mermaids try with other mermaids, or love them only anyway. But kisses just parch the lips and tits, well. They're dandy, but. Some declare they don't need anyone else. Lucky few. What else; the ones who can't deal float out, thinking. Thinking if thinking alone will tip them over the edge. Fantasies under icesheets of non-existent merboys with hard-ribbed narwhale horns and coarse, clever hands. Fantasies of mermaids with warm, green-fringed caves. Decorous fantasies of both, in all combinations, with all manner of parts: those that are absent, and parts that are new, known only to the minds of desperate dreaming fishgirls. Some drift long, letting themselves sink into the abyss, thinking, well it's symbolic, right? But all they find down there are glowing jelly brutes and wheedling prawn.

Well, how do they find out about—look, how did you find out about it?

Mermaids up top gather on the slicked rocks, shining wildly, trying to think of something to say beyond, have you found an orgasm yet? You look sleepy, are you sure you don't have anything you'd like to share with the rest of us. Not voicing the question, where exactly are we all appearing from, given even parthenogenesis is off the table? Nor anything on the logistics of shit. They pose and lounge, forks in hand, waving coyly at a gappy flotilla as each ship blares its horns like this damn parade could ever be salient. Mermaids go quiet, look at one another, swollen tails splashing. The last boat of the evening goes over the white wake and some drunk lad's singing another fucking song about salt curls and perky breasts and getting married to the sea. A grip around the foot and a long trip down into the blue. But the mermaids haven't drowned anybody in years. See, there's a step missing, between dragging a boy under and the part with the sex. So what's murder on its own, a way to get off? They aren't that twisted. And then we come back to the lacking of anything like a pleasure zone.

It's a mytho-biologically dictated trait towards chronic unfulfilment: save adding a footnote to the fables, there's nothing whatsoever that can be done. But finally, the thought occurs that there might be something hidden that they've missed. One brave sister decides she'll pick a vee from her scales, grabs a salt-reddened knife and scrabbles them off. Just to check, just to double-check. It hurts blue-green behind the eyes, but no worse than a hypothesis unconfirmed.

Underneath there's nothing but stinging salmon-pink flesh.

Not a mergirl utters a word.

She scatters her mauled scales into the water. The tide takes a hundred gleaming tickets to the party, but there just isn't the space to dance. Eventually the scales grow back, and flank her in, prim as the heads of a hundred brand-new masonry nails.

LOPE

I asked him outright. A wrinkle on his foot. Ditches where dirt stuffed them. Thinking of the Christmas turkey. The woods mushy with first snow falling into melt at once. With jerky movements my darling sliced bread. Fingers tensed against it, grip like a marble Bernini hand. I looked down, hating myself and desire.

He stopped. Put the knife on the board. Yes, he said, looking at the woods. Past the fence posts you'll find the sheep carcass spread open like a picnic blanket. I even ate the bones.

And the farmer? I asked.

Hush. A pot bubbled. I thought: don't I love how his sleeve clasps his upper arm. I love the red hair at his throat and chest. A sheen of distractions—the presents awaiting the kids, out at their grandparents. The tock of their coming, soon. My mother, my father. His long gone, or so he'd always claimed.

Leaning into me. Those arms, that thin cotton covering, mine, his. Head down. The morning snow, but thinking of the dusk trees. When I circled them with torchlight, calling.

Yes, he said. Him too.

I brought out the list from the place it is kept, handed him the pen. Let him prop the pad on my back. Days since last killed: 457, struck out. Written below: days since last killed: 1. Then the growl of a car in the drive. Then hale our red children came bounding in.

SUMMER LIGHTNING

There is something banking yellow in the sky. Still the seats in the airport face a row of windows in which a thousand faces mirror, thousands of loose bodies wander, gleaming, stripped and sampled, with their shadows left behind in their cars and straightened out under their paisley duvets. Here greys: a neat bin, a buttress. A cream glow, the opening to a perfumery.

Airports are ritual places, full of cleansing rites. The placement of papers, the purification before entry—remove your shoes, your belt. Pass through the gate if you are worthy, enter the chambers of light without time.

One man walks differently from the rest. He is barefoot. He is spitting dry beans from his mouth. A ritual from Ancient Rome. He walks steadily through thick air, and the crowd parts. Everyone except a small girl. The girl has been at the beauty counter; her mouth is spread orange, her dark eyelids dabbed green and sparkly. She steps out and puts up her hand.

An epic sound splits the air: outside the first of the lightning has struck a grounded plane. The man recognises what she is. He bows deeply at the waist and spits out a handful of dried beans, waiting for her to realise. He lets the mouthful of offerings fall to clack across the flooring tiles.

This man is here to annihilate the girl. He has tried before, over and over. He thinks she is not human, but a household ghost lacking abode. A cultural slip with a dozen faces. An affront that needs to be otherwise, neutralised. The girl smiles and her big white teeth have a gap. The man shudders.

He hunches, turns red. He draws open his mouth and a torrent of dried beans spews out. Protection, correction. In Ancient Rome, the man of the house would sprinkle broad beans around his property, warding against the *lemures*, the needy dead. He's performing same. Forcing into effect freedom from those gone unmourned, despicable, untouchable, unmoored. In this way to tell himself into being. A man of actions, him. A man with primogeniture rights. Look at him clench his jaw.

But one woman in the crowd comes forward. Her eyes are hooded and her bag is tight at her side. She's going home but her flight is delayed until the storm passes. The artificially dehumidified mugginess is choking her: she has put her scarf away, a gossamer scarf she'd chosen that morning to highlight the beauty otherwise easily missed in the plainness of her face. And still she puts a hand on the stranger's arm. *Hey, now.*

The girl is dead, or the girl is not dead, or the man has run out of beans, or he has an endless supply, or the last few are spilling to the ground, looking like tiny foetal forms. This woman, who is she, refusing room for any harm, refusing ritual, continuity, even here. Even in the airport where continuity is the only thing holding the canopy of glass above the heads of so many.

The woman takes a pamphlet out of her bag. Some words on health, on speaking to others about your sorrows. Hopelessly insufficient. But what else, anyway. Presuming he, too, is human. Above the airport the yellow banks let out a roar and a second livid fork of electricity. A small vehicle on the tarmac, carrying a train of luggage, bursts into flames. The man takes the pamphlet and glares into space. His eyes are wet and dark.

He has no action, no form to follow. The woman, the crowd, watch as he limps away, over the avenue of beans, unshadowed under the airport lighting.

The girl, the girl. She has ladybirds on her yellow dress. She smiles orange gappy and goes round in a spin so her dress does too. She doesn't have to tell you nothing. There are so many more. There are so many more in the vast hall, and everywhere, holding on brightly to the edges, while the storm, with its own agenda, answers every tension with release.

MUSEUM OF HARMS

He curated the bee room. Small china figurines, dripping. Swarm as a curtain, as a concealed vibration behind the tapestries. It served no purpose, caused no real pain, since you could walk through with great delicacy or in a terrible hurry, and the bees in their veils would never sting. There was nothing much else he could do, now that he had come back to the old place, bar this refurbishment. Some minor adjustments to the architecture to add breadth, sweep, to make it the palace of a cardinal long dead, or living still, in a world adjacent to this. Then cardamom and pear hot drink in a red tin cup. Him in crisp black, shaven, clean hair, though he never washed, never groomed, though he never changed at all.

He really ought to stay put a little while longer. He let distraction fondle the keys, asking himself: what's the difference between a super villain and a monster? Well, some choice in the matter. Some tweaks in the mechanism of secret identities. Often, though not always, a disparity in budget. He shrugged and wandered into the ballroom of disassociation, though that never threw him for long. On other occasions he imported fashion from Harajuku. Pastels, weirdly, looked best. He unpacked and smoothed the outfits on himself, looked in the long Gothic mirrors, ran a hand through angelic curls, and sighed. And went back to the usual threads.

Out upon the grounds, the ha-ha, hidden, marked the line between smooth green lawn and the onset of hell. In the same field, every hour, some picture never before seen. Flames of fleshy colours, a hail of skulls cracking against the rocks. Or the eerie quiet before the flashbacks of a war came on, a lurid aura behind the eyes.

He curated the abnormalities room and filled it with the lonely, and made it so they could not see one another, nor be heard. The poetic cliché room, decorated with imitations of Blake. The gun room, now that was taunting him. He tried to imagine a torture comparable to a gun but these were so sleekly awful all on their own. Never had people made the like, in his mind, to match a gun, nor had told so many lies about them. Or felt so strong, even as children, holding the machine like sailors clutching iron anchors as they sink.

He made the reading room full of needed words unsaid, and the worst thoughts of modest, quiet people, even if they made it to heaven. There were also plenty of novels to fill his time, because the human condition was ultimately better dried on the page and inhaled over burgundy, by the fire. He loved pathos as much as blood. Some of his favourite authors, too, had rooms of their own.

But with infinite resources, even the devil does not

know what to do with his own idle hands. He clicked on his long legs, entered the lift. There was a someone on his mind. Exit is a simple road, but long. It leads out across edgetowns, past the high flats, under bridges, by the highway, multilane greys where only crushed Coke cans, condoms, and bodies get thrown, where no one should go but a man in black, wavering slightly.

He rested a while. A packet of Ritz's crackers and a bottle of Fuji water for refreshment. He carefully made the waste into stones. It didn't do to pollute. In his pocket he found several bees nuzzled together; these he took out on his palm. The wind caught their clear wings and ruffled their fur. There was no devil of bees.

At the approach to the town he wanted, he paused. What if he was making a mistake? It had been one night. One night, and when? He looked at his long, greyscaled fingers, muttering. The dear girl was probably long dead. Yet he hadn't met her where he had expected. And after a night like that? Not that he judged on those grounds. But he had thought perhaps there'd be a mark against. Given her dancing partner.

The devil took out his abominable hand from his other pocket and looked at it open, he whose very touch corrupts, watching more of the little black bees rising, going out over the parched fields. The way it was, he thought, was how the bees sought to know by honest means what there was to be known. An aery kingdom mapped by dances, physics, sweet, fragile creation. Perhaps it wasn't quite so florid. But anyway. There was room for special blessings too small to be named.

He shuffled a few steps. Held his chin upwards and

at last spoke her name. It came out without the venomous slurring so often expected, so often performed. In kinship, nothing in the great wide world was urged towards answer.

The devil with a moment's hesitation turned and walked away smartly, headed back towards his museum.

And in secret he smiled to himself, delighted.

UNSPOKEN

Mia worked hard to be like everyone else at her school. When she thought too much about certain things in the past, vines came out of her eyes and, given a few minutes, sprouted leaves. A few sprigs at the tear ducts were okay, concealable under big bug sunglasses. But people started to almost notice if the gloss unfurled, if it began to bud and open tiny white-and-blue stars.

She waited for her eye problem to mean something. It never did. She tried sometimes to snip the leaves off; it didn't hurt. Just made a lapful of cuttings. She would pull on a jumper and go out in the fog. The school, old, creaking, was near a frequently fog-bound sea. The school was also near a park. Mia could deposit her foliage there. It worried and disgusted her though. To put pieces of herself in the bins or tossed under a shrub.

Mia waited for meaning, peering at the world from behind her glasses. Just as she would if looking for love. The fog was a good place to have these thoughts: it softened everything, even her. One day another girl caught her in the bathroom with the scissors. A girl with boy hair and a long denim shirt. What are you doing? she asked. Cutting the plants that grow from my eyes, said Mia. Easier than pulling them out. Oh yes, said the girl, craning her neck, distracted by the vista out the window. Deer on the grass again, six, all doe. The girl blinked once, rubbed her own eyes. Any idea what the homework was supposed to be for today? Mia blushed. Looked out the window in silence. Waiting for meaning to rise up and meet her. The deer herd, leaping, flashed away across the green.

TO STRING

To make a special excursion to the place where last they were seen.

To take a bus and then a train, the green countryside blipping past, the technology of an earlier era but no less miraculous.

To arrive at the station, the only person standing on the platform under a yellowing sky.

To see likewise the yellow fields of rapeseed swaying in a breeze your arms do not register.

To feel in your nerves the storm hunching below the horizon.

To depart from the station on foot and walk to the nearest signpost.

To discover the distance to your destination is four and a half miles, and choose not to wait for the rural bus.

To remove from a messenger bag of soft i.e. well-worn leather a miniature jar of honey and a ledger with a soft leather cover in a brown shade exactly matched to the messenger bag.

To adjust your glasses.

To put the honey jar in your blazer pocket, ignoring the disruption to the line of your coat.

To begin walking in the direction of your destination, while silently reading from the ledger and keeping an eye on your feet, the overgrown verge, and the unasphalted road.

To realise you have forgotten your flask of coffee on the train.

To, at length, reach your destination with a great thirst upon you.

To step up to the threshold without stopping to take in the magnitude of the premises.

To remove the jar of honey from your pocket and set it down a moment.

To remove from an inner pocket of the blazer a small pearl-handled knife.

To remove your left shoe and left sock.

To lean down and score along the sole of your foot with the knife until a thin line of blood follows the blade.

To smear the blood from the knife to the top stone of the doorstep.

To smear over this a little of the honey, so that honey and blood lie beside each other in a tiny rainbow.

To return the knife to the pocket (leaving the opened jar of honey) and to return all clothing to the order it had been in before.

To take in a long breath.

To hold that breath for one, two, three seconds before letting it out.

To rub your fingers upon which the mingled honey and blood remain in trace.

To step across the threshold.

To walk down the hall, imagining what it would have been to have been the first.

To imagine what it would have been like as the academic who first declared this site irreparably contaminated.

To imagine entering this place clean, as it was then.

To consider yourself clean, anyway, disregarding the knowledge that first academic indirectly transmitted to you and every other visitor.

To find yourself in a room which you do not remember entering.

To feel your shoe beginning to dampen.

To sit at the great stone hearth.

To be sitting at a great stone hearth that is not in the same room that you do not remember entering, but in another room altogether.

To move to another room, possibly a few.

To note: kitchen (giant oven), dining room (wax hand and wizened grapes in a glass punch bowl), sunroom (no light coming from the outside, as if all is a naked midnight, when it was just moments before the height of day), bedroom (bed small and enclosed with curtains. Bed you find yourself lying in, with your shoes dangling off the edge, grey stars in your head, you note, from a loss of blood).

To have always been squeamish, and aware that this would occur.

To know that boundaries must be made fuzzy and unstable, and that to do this might require you to become fuzzy and unstable.

To laugh in the way that people alone tend to laugh, as if their continued presence on earth depends on laughing in a way that is convincing to themselves, or potential listeners-in.

To reach a basement where you are sure the last came to, before they crossed the border, irreparably.

To have no memory of stairs beyond a new smear on your hand, of beeswax polish.

To be confused as to what constitutes a memory and what a sensation of slickness.

To be reminded of the great thirst that is upon you.

To lick your lips subconsciously, then consciously, then wipe your lips, tasting metal and honey and a secondary type of the secretions of bees.

To find a bottle of wine, very old, with an art nouveau image of a naked woman on it, and to crumble the cork with your fingers and drink the contents.

To feel immediate regret.

To wake up on the floor of the wine cellar in a wineskin of a body, something sloshing around in there.

To hear a voice.

To hear two voices.

To see, as you tilt your head, feet coming down the stair to the wine cellar.

To know that this person, who is wearing a pair of coral slippers, is not the others you came to see, but a different person entirely, and only singular. Or only two. Not enough at any rate.

To know that you have broken something.

To be confused as to whether the broken something is internal or external of your body.

To be confused as to whether you are a body, have a body, or what.

To then know that you do not have a history, or a messenger bag, or a cut on your foot (though you felt it, probably, just a few moments ago, or however long).

To know that you may not have one face, but many.

To have it confirmed, then, that the break was external, or rather not-you, since you have no interior, therefore nothing exists in relation to this interior.

To hate yourself (not-self, *whatever*).

To feel regret that you used to leave philosophy lectures early and go and buy hot chocolate to take out to the beach to watch the sunset, even though this was quite close to perfection at the time.

To know anyway you are a trope, the intruder, the unexpected guest who is in fact there to inspect.

To be aware that this is how the others must have vanished.

To feel irreparably contaminated.

To put both hands over your mouth and squeal into this closed space until this hollow terror leaves you.

To watch the feet passing you by—not just the coral-red slippered feet, but a pair of light boots that might belong to a man, given their size, a man whose job it is to travel a lot outside in unexpected climates.

To realise that the owners of the feet have not become aware of your presence, despite your prone position in the middle of the wine cellar floor.

To breathe awkwardly for a few moments, trying to arrange your face so that it is not a wax model but a human face. Metaphorically speaking.

To get unsteadily to your feet.

To look at your left shoe and see despite the odds that it has turned black-red.

To remain unseen and hyperventilating.

To stare a while at the two, one indeed a man in outdoor clothing, the other a woman of some age, but evident amounts of self-control and grace.

To at length go up the stairs, hoping to avoid losing time.

To walk into a room you have never been in before, which makes sense, since this is not the place you entered.

To sit down at a long table of fine wood in a different room, in so different a style again that it might be a room in another century, or at least in the house of a person overly keen on historical re-enactments of great verisimilitude.

To break down crying, a really just all-out, orgasmic sort of crying.

To suddenly come upon another room.

To suddenly come upon another, this one filled with young adults, all of exceptional beauty and breezy gormlessness, staring back at you.

To come upon another room. Or it is the same room, but so utterly changed.

To blink.

To still find the walls of that room coated in a rust liquor, as they were a moment ago.

To look down at scraps of white clothing, nothing much else: black-and-white tile; smeared prints; wood; cork; sand; terracotta; your two shoes, one brown, the other black-red.

To hold your face in your hands.

To feel your teeth strange in your mouth.

To feel your lips chapped from the red wine and other substances.

To feel a great weight on the top of your head.

To feel with your fingers the weight is coming from a ribbed absence in the air above your scalp.

To start laughing, not trying to convince yourself of anything anymore, but laughing until your heart squeezes uncomfortably in your chest.

To, at length, desist from laughing.

To find your breathing awkward, but continuous.

To find with your descending, empty, sticky fingers your glasses still there on the bridge of your nose.

To take a little comfort in that.

SCIENCE

Oil in the chimney catches alight. The engine hisses. You step off a platform. I hide in your luggage, a scrap, a fold beneath your white shirts and black braces, neat. Your tooth in an envelope to me, and back this toothless growth from my brain, a spare. Dear creator, your wretch misses you too. I am in the North. Your train cannot traverse even a frozen sea. Images stickle. The ferry. The greys melting like afterburn. How can I live alone and unconsidered. I demanded a girl for my usage. Let me down at the window of your sea berth. In my growth: bile demands. Secretions. See, this. This is what you bring about when you refuse me. I'd like to sow myself. I'd like to damp another body open with my parts. The monster is a leery bulge. But more: a hunger, trudging across its own bitterness.

And we have the same face. Your moustaches, waxed, so prim above your lips. Mine lopsided because you forgot to show me how to shave. You are slowly narrowing our distance. This is narrative. Embark in sealskin and eider across the shifts of the ice. Blue-green warp overhead. When we meet, you let me live because you, too, are a man. Blood crush. I pull out my lovelessness in the form of my cock, and we take measurements. This is customary.

How many will be dead. Hubris, burnished like gold. Icebreaker and sledge. How many more stars but none more than we shall know. The dogs leap forward only to freeze. Necks arched. The ice pulls their gums back over their teeth. When you find me you love me you know me.

Always the cold and your staggering, admitting only now, at the very end; you brush my ice-scabbed scars. The frost stars still left, and us. This will, always, onwards.

TABLESCAPES!

The actors sit waiting for their host to finish plating up.

Out of sight of the cameras, the audience, everyone, six dolls made of clay have been hammered into the dining table. There is the sound of the ocean when the actors open their mouths, which is whenever they are required to speak to the host.

The host is a smiling lady with blonde hair and blue, vein-shot eyes that don't quite focus, and lipgloss that slides in a similar way, but a frosted brownish pink.

"And now a little garnish. I love to use basil as garnish, it's just so pretty?" The host leans over to deliver each sprig. She brings over the plates. The food is brown, the food is steaming. The food is other colours and textures, recognisably something like food. The actors cut up everything on their plates. The actress laughs at something the host says. She pulls a glass up to her mouth. She talks about her next role. She looks at the actor to her right, and he begins to gesticulate at the food and make appreciative noises.

"Night salad," another actor says. The crowd laugh.

Next up, an easy twist on an old favourite that you can do at home, that you can do all by yourself. If you can open a bag of chips you can do it. The food on the table disappears. The actors get up and all of them go away, except for the woman and the man who had been to her right. The host says nothing. The two actors then disappear.

Now it is Thanksgiving, now the set is her home, with red and gold trees outside, and festive turkey decorations. And lots of dried corncobs in a garland of wicker and noxious leaves.

"I just love Thanksgiving?" says the host. "Pumpkin spice. And this is a little something extra you can do real quick." She turns round to a child coming in from the garden. The child is carrying more festive turkey decorations in a cute basket.

"Yeah, good job."

She takes out a tiny bow and arrow from a display. She aims the arrow at the child's throat and pulls back. A flurry of crow feathers. Slime from a pond pumping behind. The child's eyes roll up and he grins and falls to the floor. The host picks up the basket and balances it under one arm, smiling at the camera.

"It's Jjusrt such a speshihal tiem yeeeraa," the host says, "famurly."

After the commercial break it's time for tablescapes.

Tablescapes!

The Christmas tree is covered in upside-down martini glasses. Somewhere a crow is naked and throwing itself against a basement window. A good guess would be the bathroom. The host pouts at the camera. She winks. The host is in a furry sweater that says *SANTAN HO HO HO* on it, but the letters are fuzzy.

"My grandson," the host says.

The home dining room is a dark maroon. Christmas music is playing; when it is playing it is too slow, it is sludging, too slow for Bing Crosby, and the glass in the basement window has cracked. Fake snow is getting inside. Bloodied tiny bird on the floor of the bathroom, behind the toilet.

The camera pans over to the table. The host is standing behind a chair. There are no guests; she is pretending later there will be guests.

"Tablescapes!" she says. "My friends love 'em. I made this

blanket," the host says, narrowing her eyes happily and flicking back her hair. There is a blanket over the table. TADAAH. The host whips off the blanket.

Underneath is.
Underneath is a body.

The camera pans over the body. The damage is very old. There are white rice grains crawling over the body.

"So affordable!" says the host. "I spent years learning how to get the technique just right. Now so can you."

Ribs spike. Drip. Oh, tinsel. Knives and forks, and this special cutlery is just right for serving things in aspic. The host moves over to the wall. Her fingernails are shiny. Her lips smile like they are the lips of another person who doesn't know her very well. Her teeth pry the lips. Metallic and covered in wine.

She flicks the switch.

"It's alive!" she says, as the red and green bulbs light up, inside the corpse.
"Haha, just a lil' bit of something you can do at home with things you have lying around."

The lead for the coloured lights has been carefully tucked away, held with invisible tape.
The host pulls out a bottle of red wine. The bottle of wine is mostly empty. She tips it in any glass and raises it up.

"And I wish you a merry. And to all."
The host invites you to come back any time to her home.
The music intensifies. A light buzzes red and bone, until
something causes it to stop.

A SHORT HISTORY
OF CREATION

The shack on the hillside has been left with the solar porch light on. Miguel is grateful as he makes his way towards it while rocks catch his unsteady feet. Around him, thickets of thorny brush, snakes and spiders in their shallow dens. Maybe they should bite him, get him done with. But the tiny light is always fixed ahead of him in the blue murk.

The shack was his grandfather's, a base built for specking gold. Miguel will make it there for dawn. Collapse onto a board bed, sleep until midday. There's a well at the back that will have water for months. He can trap rabbits; he is bringing a guide to know what plants, if any, are good to eat—he can live. It's not like he is a child anymore; he's fourteen. But there isn't much consolation in all of this. Not now that he has murdered two people.

Miguel turns to look back at the flatland from where he has come. The turgid river runs silver, cleaned up by the moonlight. The few buildings of the shopping strip stand out, and the string of lights marking the railway station. Is anyone down there awake to know he's fled? He rubs grit from his eye and moves on, scrambling, stumbling, cursing, but not loud enough to alert anyone below.

It started because he drew real things instead of things that had come from his imagination. It started because early that summer his neighbour Maggie gave him pencils, pad, and her old Leica, and he decided he'd take pictures of the gum trees on the edge of the garden, where the river ran. He wasted a whole roll of film; close-ups of the bark, the way the sun came through branches late in the day.

All of the trees then died. Overnight. His family said it was the drought. And Miguel believed them. But the river, as thick and scummy as it was, still brought water to the banks.

After the trees, he drew rocks and the flowers he stole out of plant pots—of course these died; he'd picked them and left them in the heat. He showed his pictures to Maggie, and she took one, had it framed for her wall. Then she asked if he'd like to paint her, so she could put that up on the wall too, next to the photo of her husband.

The oils were the richest thing Miguel had ever touched. Painting took a week. Maggie would come peering round, chatting away, suggesting some tweaks to the palette or the angles. On the day it was done, Miguel lifted it off the easel and brought it round to her armchair. It was just what Maggie wanted. A bobby-dazzler, she said. Something to celebrate. But getting up to fetch the tea things, the old woman staggered. She pressed a weak hand to her head. On her fingers a thick, oily, colourful blot. But Maggie never wore makeup, and she had no paint on her. She looked at her hand, perplexed, and then at Miguel. And fell down awkwardly. And wouldn't get up. There was an odd, colourless pit marked into her temple, where her hand had brushed the skin.

Miguel couldn't believe he'd actually killed his neighbour. So he went on taking photos of shadows and sun, sketches of fields that soon withered. Trying to improve, since that's what old Maggie would have wanted him to do. November turned to December. Christmas was a blazing blur. Then January came, and his sister returned home from London with a Polaroid camera and some retro film. He posed her against the turquoise wall of the house and pressed the big orange button with his thumb.

He'd only wanted a picture of her to have when she was away.

Up in the shack, Miguel drops into a deep stagnant nothing. He wakes, makes chicken ramen on the portable stove. The day wears on miserably. He feels ill, alone, not sure how to sort the slurry of his feelings. Towards dusk nausea hits and Miguel takes his dry heaving outside. He sits for a bit, thinking of nothing. The wind drops. The sun starts to set. There's a pinky gold light, and a flock of rosy galahs chipping through the air.

Then he thinks of his sister, lying somewhere cold, and her skin turning brighter and fading like instant film. He thinks of his mum and dad, staring emptily over her. An aneurysm, that's what they were told, could have happened at any time. Drought, a blood vessel bursting in the brain. Maggie, they'd said, had a weakness in her skull, even a light fall would have caved it in.

It's getting too hard to see. It's too hard to see, and Miguel is sobbing.

After a while, the boy walks to the well and pulls up the bucket. He refills his bottle then pours the rest down the hill, knowing this is another crime. He pours the whole bucket over the earth. Then he fetches a second. He pours until the bodies wash away. Until the drought's over. Until the fields burst, rich and green and permanent.

The moon's up again now, putting polish to the spill. But Miguel's eyes are dark. He stands watching over what he has made, until the earth soaks up the light.

SŌPHROSYNĒ

The collective sits in the clearing in the country park, between the ancient oaks, awaiting instruction. There is something stirring this spring morning. The silver birches on the edge of the oak field hiss, and the sound of the river comes up from the ravine. The manuscript on the bench flaps noisily under a paperweight. The elected reader is checking something on her phone. That's the hour, she says.

In the early part of the last century, this park was estate land of a major duchy. Everyone in the collective has some tie to the family name, as scion or servant. The war may have struck down the direct heirs and commandeered the castle for barracks and Cold War machinations, but even now the collective remains, forbidden to sever connection, forbidden to speak of what it is they are called to perform.

The beat of a drum starts up, setting the pace for the ceremony. The collective stands in formation. Someone's phone starts to ring and another whispers angrily for them to turn it off. The hissing of the birches changes gradually, until other sounds can be differentiated. The clicking of cloven hooves. The white deer are coming.

It was Michaelmas Day, 1698, favoured by fine weather. The duke, his friends and serving men went out hunting, riding down corridors of beech, into the thickets where the charcoal smokers were at work, over the heaps of ancient earthworks and on into the wildwoods.

Even then, the oaks were very old, and had cleared a space between their great trunks where nothing but primroses grew, in season or out. A gallery of huge trees with bulbous bodies and holes deep enough to fit a man's arm. The hounds reached the clearing first. There came a terrible din. When the barks of his hounds turned to a high-pitched yelping, the duke did not stop to think, but kicked his horse into a swift canter.

A multitude of white deer stood amongst the oaks. The dogs had fled. What the duke did, in his haste, was a sin so great that it could not be forgotten by time. So great that even those who had no claim to the privileges of his name, but were merely locked in servitude, would be as much afflicted as the highest-born. Girl children and boy would be forever tied to that moment, on a fine Michaelmas Day, 1698.

The duke aimed his bow at the throat of the largest stag, a beast with antlers of such a span it would have given most folkf pause. Let it not be said that the duke was a wise man. Afterwards the others, servants and nobles alike, gathered, and all were agreed that there was, as there had been in the first King David's time, a flicker of godliness above its head, and that the eyes held some severe kind of intelligence, though of what nature they could not agree.

But the duke had room in his mind only for hunting, hunger and wrath. He drew out his sword to finish the hart, and grabbing the antlers at the root, beheaded it. Only then did he pull back the reins of his horse. A great horror had come over him. The stag's head had separated from the body with as much ease as a pear cut with a knife. The duke raised the head—and saw that it looked at him still. The head began to bay.

And every other stag in the gallery tilted back his head and answered with a cry like the yowling from a Carnyx, a war-horn. Like the madness of a war. As if calling for the hunt to continue. In the distance, the pack of scattered dogs howled their return.

The head began to melt. It poured white and glossy down the duke's arm, down his horse's leg. The horse screamed and started, throwing the duke from the saddle. On the ground among the unseasonable primroses, the duke went pale and fainted completely away. His men carried him back to the castle and laid him in his bed.

He wouldn't die just then. In fact, he would live a long life. He would see his money sunk into the mire of the colony of Darien, which hovered into brief calamitous existence at the end of that year, in distant Panama. Near ruined, the duke would sign away his country's independence so as to avoid the loss of his duchy. His descendants would become the forefront of the British Empire, indulging their hungers and wraths upon the Americas, India, Africa, the Caribbean.

And each Michaelmas the heirs of the name and the

connected servants were bound to return to the gallery, to atone to the herd, which came also. The method of atonement was written by the duke on a manuscript, in Scots. He instructed the collective to gather to witness the coming of the strange white deer; that they must bring some nice fruit and things that deer also like, which he had determined were well-crafted or natural items of a white colour. Shells and glassware and tiny china deer. These would be put into the holes in the oak, in front of the stags, and some prayers said. Not prayers to God, but to the beasts themselves, whatever they might be.

It was said because of this offering the family flourished. Tobacco and sugar and bodies almost without number were theirs. Then wars came, the lands fell. The stags were not expected to explain. The ritual was explanation enough.

The drummer drums, the stags appear. The trinkets are hidden away. The prayers are said. And history is chained to the quivering body. History was committed, is not to be torn from. No one thinks to halt the process to see what the deer might do. A pale green leaf falls to the ground unnoticed. Things pass, and ache in their ambiguity to be understood.

Michaelmas Day, long after the first sighting, and the first cruelty. The deer return to the deeper woods. Blue sky spreads above the collective, with a cross, a white flash over it, as sometimes happens, as planes are sometimes seen to make.

EACH-UISGE

He sat among the rocks cleaning his catch, or his gathering, as it was: swirling each mussel about the water bucket, picking off fronds and bits of whisker, before transferring it with a satisfying plock into the red pail at his heel. He enjoyed working his hands through the cold, letting his mind wander. At the same time leaving space to calculate the routes of clouds travelling in the mountains that made the sea loch's edge. There was also his hunger, growing since the dawn had washed him up, fishless, driven to pickings. Salt in his beard and slimy grit in the soles of his Wellingtons.

It was a gradual realisation, amongst all this, that he was not alone.

The boy sat away only a few metres off on one of the bigger rocks where the water was rounding itself in. He was shirtless, skin white to translucence. The bones of his ribs and spine showed lightly, though the arm and the one extended leg—toe pointed in the water—were strong, wired with muscle. From the swimming. He wore a pair of pale pink boxers, veined and clinging. He was facing the water, but surely the other would be visible on his periphery. A second skin lay on a rock behind him: a wetsuit recently peeled and set to dry.

"Some day for it," he called to the newcomer, trying to keep hesitancy out of his voice.

"Aye."

The thing was not to overtalk. That was always it. He might bring up the month—February—the usual reluctance folk had for taking a dip at near zero. Make a joke, the right sort of joke. Instead he looked at the boy a little more carefully. Not a boy. Age indeterminable, but pleasingly boyish. Sometimes it was hard for him to judge. On the white skin across the shoulders, a smatter of freckles. On the face a day or two of stubble, and the eyes, crow-feeted, glancing his way, were pale with a dark limbal ring. He would do.

He rose and went to inspect the wetsuit. At first without touching. It was mussel-black, so perfect a garment to hug a body tight.

—

Bracing, that's what it was. It never got old, to be braced by the loch, and solitude, and waiting until the last advisable moment. What a morning, cool, the water with a fine bite to it. Mist in the hills, and no one else, and now, this opportunity. He had been eyeing the man at work ever since rising from the water. It had been maybe fifteen minutes, and he hadn't tired yet of looking. A handsome guy alright, though weren't they both. The manner intense, but easy, the focus of someone who knew what they must do and would do it until done well. Full dark beard with a dab of grey at the mouth. He watched as the man took off his hat and folded it before he put it in his pocket. He watched him stand and come nearer.

Now it seemed he was at a disadvantage: only the thin boxers gave him any kind of shield. The fisher was fully clothed and had a nice jumper on under his windbreaker; an old gift, worn at the cuffs from use but fitting still, a bracken-red colour. The dark hair was unruly from the hat. The man roughed his hand through it, though it seemed like the hair would go where it liked.

He shifted on the rock and tried not to adjust the clammy fabric, or react much at all. The man looked down at the wetsuit on the rock. The other pressed his head against his knee until his cheekbones hurt. Thinking, look at me, look at me. The fisher had doe-eyes, dark like the beard.

"This make any good?"

"Aye, I think so."

He answered, then— "You after a swim? You're welcome to try it on. If you want."

"Fff."

He still hadn't looked at him.

"It wouldnae fit me."

The boy watched a lock of hair shift on the man's head.

"I dunno, I dunno."

"If you think so."

"I do think so."

—

Why was he doing this? He didn't need a wetsuit, not for any reason. Was this the way it was going to be, whenever he took a fancy to some lad? If he'd any power over himself he'd wish for a bit more subtlety. He stood on one leg and removed the boot and the socks and bundled the socks into that boot. Set that bare foot on the grey sand and raised the other leg to repeat the action. The eyes of the other were on him, which meant, at least, interest. He removed his upper clothing. Then the waterproof over-trews, then the trousers themselves, which he folded. Onto a rock with these. He looked down at his naked legs and feet, thinking they were so hairy he might have been looking at animal legs. The wetsuit was tight and squealed as he pulled it over his ankles.

"Am I going about this the right way?"

"You needing a hand?"

Both legs, and then up around the waist. The hanging skin. And then the arms. It zipped in the back, so he feigned inability. Thinking of those fingers at the small of his back, touch me. The metal press, the sound of the zip, and the calm waves coming in and out. He could smell the water and the seaweed on the boy, no other personal smell. The neck tightened in. The other lingered a moment before releasing his hand, which he moved to the shoulder.

"It's not too tight?"

He raised an arm and lowered it. He looked at the boy, very close now. Freckles on his eyelids. He would do. Held behind the neoprene, his stomach gurgled.

"As it should be, I think."

—

There was that intensity. It was all glances off to the side, sharp intakes of breath. Well, at least he wasn't alone in this. In the low times. He drew the hair back from his face and met the gaze, just. They were miles from anywhere.

"We'll have a try-out, shall we? Then see about going somewhere to get warm."

"Is it that bad?"

No, it's not that bad."

"Alright. A few laps."

First one man and then the other walked towards the sea. Walked, led, followed each other with hands held out, into the glassy water, among the clots of rust-coloured seaweeds. And down. And under. And gone.

ACKNOWLEDGEMENTS

Thank you to all the people who told me to be better, who generously read, critiqued or shared my writing or otherwise kept me on track: Katherine Angel, Dr Gill Best, Dr Paul Dawson, Kathy Fish, Casey Hannan, Steve Himmer, Jimmy Kelly, Kirsty Logan, Cari Luna, Chris J. Rice, and Michael Schmidt. Thank you to Miguel Marquez for lending me his name. Gratitude is also and of course due in abundance to Queen's Ferry Press and Erin McKnight.

And finally, kind thanks to The Banff Centre and Creative Futures Scotland, whose generosity created room for the forests in these stories.

Helen McClory is a writer from Scotland. She has a PhD in Creative Writing from the University of Glasgow and an MA in Creative Writing from the University of New South Wales. There is a moor and a cold sea in her heart. This is her first collection.

Lightning Source UK Ltd.
Milton Keynes UK
UKOW08f1553270417
300035UK00002B/37/P